31241008483375

OCT - - 2015

Nanny X Returns

Nanny X Returns

Madelyn Rosenberg

illustrations by
Karen Donnelly

Holiday House / New York

Library of Congress Cataloging-in-Publication Data

Rosenberg, Madelyn, 1966-
Nanny X returns / by Madelyn Rosenberg. — First edition.
pages cm
Sequel to: Nanny X.
Summary: Alison, Jake, and their undercover nanny are on the trail of an artist
who is threatening the president and planning to destroy national treasures in
Washington, D.C.
ISBN 978-0-8234-3533-3 (hardcover)
[1. Nannies—Fiction. 2. Brothers and sisters—Fiction. 3. Undercover operations—
Fiction. 4. Spies—Fiction. 5. Mystery and detective stories. 6. Washington (D.C.)—
Fiction.] I. Title.
PZ7.R71897Nd 2015
[Fic]—dc23
2015004324

For Sally

Acknowledgements

HQ: Mary Cash and the fine folks at Holiday House

Secret agents: Susan Cohen and Nora Long

Intelligence: Graham Lazorchak, Karina Lazorchak, Breece Walker, Moira Rose Donohue, Jacqueline Jules and Wendy Shang

The Usual Suspects: Tom, Cece, Mary, Molly, Rachael, Anamaria, Andrew, Mel, Jules, Mom, Jimmy, Dad, Linda, Sally, Marfé, Marty, Carla, Ann, Anna, Laura and Liz

The Unusual Suspects: One More Page, Politics and Prose, Sara Lewis Holmes, Mr. Schu, Margie, Library Laura, Jama and This Kid Erik

Maps and Legends: Karen Donnelly

Secret Passwords: George Newman

Segway Training: Chester Eng

Strategic Planning and Vehicular Operations: Butch Lazorchak

Map of the National Mall

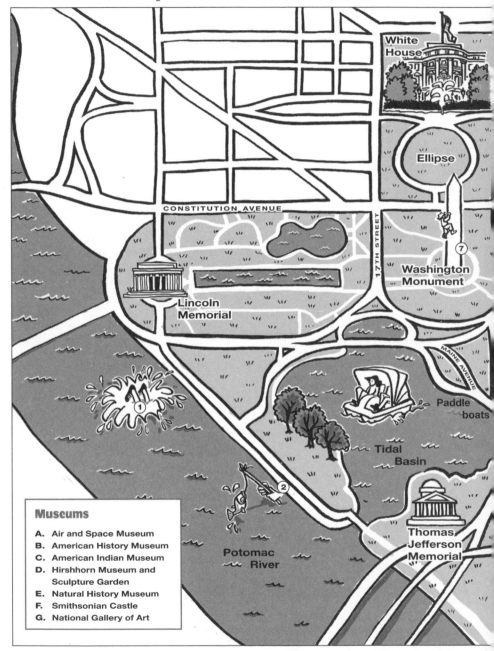

Museums

A. Air and Space Museum
B. American History Museum
C. American Indian Museum
D. Hirshhorn Museum and Sculpture Garden
E. Natural History Museum
F. Smithsonian Castle
G. National Gallery of Art

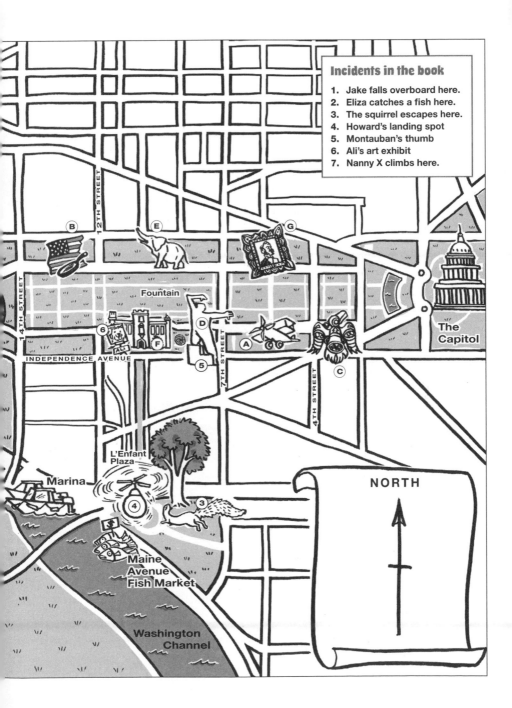

Incidents in the book

1. Jake falls overboard here.
2. Eliza catches a fish here.
3. The squirrel escapes here.
4. Howard's landing spot
5. Montauban's thumb
6. Ali's art exhibit
7. Nanny X climbs here.

ALSO BY *Madelyn Rosenberg*

Nanny X

Contents

1. Alison: Nanny X Returns 1

2. Jake: Nanny X Tries on a New Hat 5

3. Alison: Nanny X Has a Man Overboard 10

4. Jake: Nanny X Gets Some Help from a Purple Minnow 15

5. Alison: Nanny X Reels One In 20

6. Jake: Nanny X Gets Held Up by a Squirrel 24

7. Alison: Nanny X Grabs the Remote 30

8. Jake: Nanny X Gets Some Help from a Chimp 34

9. Alison: Nanny X Takes a Nap 38

10. Jake: Nanny X Heads for the White House 43

11. Alison: Nanny X Is Out of the Picture 48

12. Jake: Nanny X Reads Some Poetry 53

13. Alison: Nanny X Knows Her Alphabet 57

14. Jake: Nanny X Holds the Bag 61

15. Alison: Nanny X Skates Right By 65

16. Jake: Nanny X Learns Some History 72

17. Alison: Nanny X Sets the Trap 76

18. Jake: Something's Bugging Nanny X 80

19. Alison: Nanny X Learns About Insect Digestion 84

20. Jake: Nanny X Goes Rock Climbing 89

21. Alison: Nanny X Puts a Fork in it 96

Name the Artwork 98

Nanny X's Skating Tip No. 12: How to Stop 99

1. Alison

Nanny X Returns

I thought we'd get a new case the second Nanny X walked back into our living room wearing her motorcycle jacket and mirrored sunglasses. But she didn't say anything about a new case. She didn't even say anything about an old case. Instead, she acted like it was just a normal day and like she was a normal nanny, instead of an agent for NAP—Nanny Action Patrol.

I went for the direct approach, which is one of my specialties. "Do you have a new case we can help you with?"

"You may help me set the table," said Nanny X. "You may also help solve The Case of the Dog Who Needed to Be Walked."

Our dog's name is Yeti, after the abominable snowman, but he's not even a little abominable. I walked him, super fast, and when I came back inside, my brother had taken over The Case of the Ordinary Nanny.

"When are you going to get a new hat?" Jake asked her.

"I didn't know you were interested in fashion, Jake Z," said Nanny X.

On her first and best day of work, Nanny X had worn a straw gardening hat with pink flowers that served as antennas or radar or something. But she'd given it away to a chimp. You'd think she would have replaced it, if there was more work to do.

Maybe all of the crimes in Lovett, Virginia, had been solved and the only work Nanny X had left was taking care of me, Jake and our baby sister, Eliza. Or maybe there was something Nanny X wasn't telling us.

"Nanny X?" I said Friday morning after our parents had rushed off to work, gulping coffee like it was oxygen.

"Yes, Alison?"

"What's going on?"

"Life is going on," she said. "Electrical currents are usually on. The toaster, as it happens, is also on." Nanny X grabbed a piece of toast and added a thin layer of jam.

"That's not what I meant," I said. "I meant when are we going to *do* something?"

"We are going to catch the school bus in seven minutes."

"That's not what I meant, either," I grumbled.

Nanny X looked at me like she had no idea what I was talking about. My parents had given me the same look when I told them everything we'd done with Nanny X that first afternoon. I thought it was best to tell them the truth: that we'd spent the day chasing a diamond smuggler. And when they didn't quite believe me? I thought that was for the best, too.

Jake and I grabbed our backpacks while Nanny X put Eliza into the stroller. Then our nanny grabbed a diaper. I searched for the familiar silver buttons, hoping that it was a secret phone, but it wasn't. Nanny X stuck the diaper into her bag.

"Ready for your math test?" she asked me. I hadn't told her I had one; she just knew. At first I thought it was spooky that she knew so much about us. Now I wanted her to know more, like how much we wanted a new assignment.

"Make sure you reread problem No. 7," she said. "And don't forget: Your grandmother's coming tonight and you need to straighten your room when you come home. Throwing dirty clothes in the closet does not count as straightening."

The bus hissed up. "I'll see you at 3:41," Nanny X said. "On the nose."

Stinky Malloy was already on the bus, wearing his yellow safety-patrol belt. "How's Nanny X?" he asked. His nanny, Boris, was a member of NAP, too.

"Normal," I told him.

"Normal-normal or normal for Nanny X?"

"Normal-normal," I said.

"Oh," said Stinky. "That's too bad."

School was just as ordinary as home was. The only almost interesting thing that happened was during my math test. I went back to double-check problem No. 7 like Nanny X had suggested. Sure enough, my brain had burped on that question. I blew away eraser dust and fixed my answer just as Ms. Bertram called, "Time."

The bus dropped us off at precisely 3:41. We were walking home with Nanny X when her phone rang—her regular phone, not her diaper phone, which had actually blown up on our last assignment.

"Hello, Mrs. P." She didn't call our mother "Gloria" or

"Mrs. Pringle" like everybody else. "What? That's terrible. How did it happen?"

With her mirrored sunglasses, I couldn't see enough of Nanny X's face to know if the news was somebody-just-died terrible or we're-having-fish-for-dinner terrible. She must have seen me watching her, because she held up her hand like a crossing guard: *Wait.*

"No," she said. "Nothing that can't be changed. Yes. Abso-tootly. I'll let them know right away."

She hung up. "Your grandmother," she began, and I held my breath until she finished, "broke her leg in Zumba class.

"She'll be fine," Nanny X continued, "but she's in the hospital for observation. Your parents are going to Newport News to check on her. So instead of your grandmother coming to your house for the weekend, you're stuck with me instead."

Jake grinned. Apparently he had forgotten how boring the last few days with Nanny X had been.

"Tut!" said Eliza, which is her word for "stuck." She's not so good with the "*st*" or "*k*" sounds yet.

Our parents hurried home and packed their bags while Nanny X went to her own apartment to "gather a few necessities."

She came back with a small plaid suitcase and a pair of pink bunny slippers. Even I grinned when I saw what else she'd brought with her: a brand-new hat. I hoped there would be a new adventure to go along with it.

2. Jake

Nanny X Tries on a New Hat

I don't pay attention to clothes, but I would have noticed Nanny X's new hat no matter what. It was a fishing hat with lots of hooks and feathers, plus some lures that were shaped like minnows. Also, the hat was bright orange. That's good if you are trying to blend in with an orange grove. It's not so good if you are trying to be inconspicuous, which was one of my old reading-connection words. It means "not noticeable," and it's an important thing to be if you're a special agent.

Nanny X wasn't worried about being inconspicuous in our living room. She plunked down her suitcase and the bunny slippers.

"Arf," Yeti said. "Arf-arf-arf-arf-arf."

Nanny X took off her mirrored sunglasses and gave him a look. Ali says that Nanny X must have taken dog-training classes. I think she took classes in mind control instead, because Yeti stopped barking and lifted a paw to give Nanny X a high five.

"Here's my mother's room number at the hospital," my mom was saying. "And here's our cell phone number, and the pediatrician, the dentist and Jake's baseball coach. And here's a list of people you can call if there's an emergency." I bet Nanny X had her own list of people to call in case of an emergency, but I didn't say anything.

"They'll be fine, Gloria," my dad said. "Right, team?"

He waved from the passenger seat while my mom, who is a better driver, backed out of the driveway.

"What next?" I asked Nanny X.

"Dinner and then bed."

"*Bed?*" That was not the answer Ali and I were looking for. But sure enough, right after dinner that's where Nanny X sent us.

"But it's a Friday night!" Ali said. She had a growl in her voice, but she'd been growly all week so it was hard to tell if this was a new mad or just a leftover.

"The early bird catches the worm," Nanny X said, and turned out the lights.

She wasn't kidding—about being early birds or about the worms. It was darkish when she woke us up, but in the light of the kitchen she showed us a tub that said Weinrib's Premium Quality Canadian Night Crawlers. I wondered if it was one of her special gadgets. But when I opened the lid, I saw a bunch of worms wriggling around in a handful of dirt.

"That," said Ali, "is disgusting."

"Then we won't count baiting hooks among your many talents," Nanny X said. She seemed cheerful, which made me realize that she'd been a little growly all week, too.

The dark had turned to gray when we climbed into Nanny X's van, which was nothing like the kind of van a special agent would drive. She had some fuzzy dice hanging from the rearview mirror, and a canoe on the roof.

"Where are we going?" Ali asked as Nanny X buckled Eliza into a car seat.

"Downtown," said Nanny X.

"Downtown" is what people around here call Washington, D.C., which is only about ten minutes away from our house in Lovett, as long as there aren't a bunch of other cars on the road. At that time of the morning, there weren't any. Soon we were standing on the bank of the Potomac River with our canoe beside us. I wondered how sturdy it was.

"Don't worry," Nanny X said. "You'll be wearing a life jacket."

I guess she knew swimming was not one of my special talents; sinking was. At the pool, I was still in the Tadpole Group. My friend Ethan was a Shark.

We strapped on our life jackets and helped Nanny X shove the canoe into the water. Yeti sat in the front like a mermaid statue on a pirate ship. Except his hair stuck out all over instead of just flowing out of his head. Plus, his tail did not have a fishy shape.

Nanny X loaded Eliza's stroller and dropped the diaper bag next to it. It made a *Mooooooooooooooo* when it landed. Ali smiled for the first time all morning when she heard it. The sound was from *Moo, Sweet Cow* the noisiest book ever written and one of Nanny X's secret weapons.

It was a sign.

"I knew it!" I said as Nanny X used a paddle to push us off. She handed the other paddle to Ali. "This is more than a fishing trip, isn't it?"

"There are fishing trips," Nanny X said, "and there are *fishing* trips."

"So we have a case?" asked Ali, who might have been holding her breath a little.

"We have a case," said Nanny X. "We would have had it sooner, but HQ said they wanted a nanny who had more experience with fish. 'I know fish,' I told them. 'Hoo boy, do I know fish.' Then they said they wanted a nanny who could blend in. 'I blend,' I said. 'Like a chameleon, I blend.' Finally they said we could have the case. It's a big one. It concerns the president."

She gave us these details: Earlier in the week, someone going by the name of The Angler sent a note to the president with a fishhook inside it. The note came with a giant package, and in the package was a giant fish. A sculpted fish, not a real one.

"How big?" I asked.

"This big," said Nanny X. She raised one arm over her head. Then she went back to paddling.

I used to think an angler was somebody who studied angles, until I found out from Ethan that it was someone who fishes. Plus, it could be someone who thinks up crazy schemes. Ethan does both of those things. I wondered if the new bad guy did, too.

"The sculpture is described as being nine feet tall and made out of copper," Nanny X said. "The note contained instructions. And a threat."

"What kind of instructions?" I asked. I knew we were in deeper water because I could see seaweed and things. What I couldn't see was the bottom.

"What kind of threat?" asked Ali.

Nanny X answered both of us. "The Angler wants the sculpture to be installed on the White House lawn and treated like a national treasure. If it's not installed by noon today…" She paused. "If it is not installed by noon, The Angler says that some of the nation's greatest treasures will be in jeopardy."

"Be in jeopardy how?" said Ali. "Jeopardy" is a reading-connection word that means "at risk or in danger."

Nanny X shrugged. "The note didn't say."

"Why don't they just put the sculpture on the lawn?" I asked. "They have lots of empty space." Plus, a fish sculpture would be a lot more interesting than a bunch of roses.

"The president must not succumb to threats," said Nanny X. "Otherwise, think of what other people will try to do. Blackmail. Extortion. Not to mention the fact that the White House lawn could end up looking like Lulu's Cement Garden." Lulu's was a shop in Lovett that sold fountains and birdbaths, plus twelve-foot chickens. I thought it was a very interesting shop. I guess the president didn't agree. Neither did Nanny X.

"Shouldn't we be guarding something?" Ali said. "Like the art museum or the Declaration of Independence?"

"Guards we have," said Nanny X. "It isn't noon yet. If he's calling himself The Angler, he may be fishing at this very moment. I'd like to catch him before he strikes." She steered the boat close to Roosevelt Island, where the current wasn't as strong. Then she put down her paddle and pulled out a night crawler. "As long as we're here," she said, "who wants to go first?"

3. Alison

Nanny X Has a Man Overboard

Be careful what you wish for.

That's what my parents always say. I'd wished and wished that we could be on a new assignment with Nanny X. And now here we were in a canoe on the Potomac, way earlier than I ever wake up on Saturday morning, staring into a tangle of pink worms.

At least we had a case. But why did it take NAP so long to give it to us? Maybe they had decided, like the CIA, that Nanny X was getting too old for the special-agent business. Maybe they'd decided Nanny X wasn't good enough. Or what if the problem wasn't Nanny X? What if it was us?

I didn't want to believe it, but the possibility stuck to me, like dog hair on a sweater. The only way to unstick it was to solve the case. Fast.

"Don't you think The Angler will be watching the White House?" I said. "To see if the president installs the statue?"

"Possibly," she said. "But let's look at what we know. The Angler is an artist whose work features a fish. Artists like to be near the things that inspire them. You should know that, Alison."

It was true. One of my paintings had just been chosen for an outdoor exhibit on the National Mall, which is not a place where people shop, by the way, but an open space in D.C. with lots of museums and monuments. I'd submitted a painting of Yeti for the exhibit. When I had to fill out the part about what inspired me, I wrote: "I am inspired by the people and animals that I see every day." If The Angler was inspired by fish, maybe we *were* in the right place.

"My theory is that The Angler would want to stay close to the White House in order to carry out his threat," Nanny X said. "The Potomac is a mile from the White House— and from museums that are stuffed with treasures. I believe The Angler is close by. Waiting."

My mind was already making a list of treasures that could be at risk: The National Gallery of Art had paintings by loads of famous people. Abraham Lincoln's hat and Kermit the Frog were in the Museum of American History. The books in the Library of Congress were treasures. So were the cherry trees near the Tidal Basin, and themselves the other monuments.

Nanny X pressed a night crawler onto her hook and cast her line into the water. She let it dangle there and handed the container to Jake, who baited his hook and handed the night crawlers to me.

"No, thanks," I said.

"I know they're not your cup of tea, Alison," said Nanny X, which made me think about night crawlers squirming around in a teacup, which was disgusting. "Why don't you try tying some flies?"

Flies sounded even worse than worms. But instead of handing me a tub of flies, Nanny X reached into a tackle box and handed me a book: *Fly-Tying for Beginners* by Buzz Bachelder. Then she handed me a bag of feathers, a hook, a gripper-thingy and a spool of thick black thread. The idea was to tie the feathers to the hook and make it look like a real insect. Only none of the flies in the book looked like insects I'd seen before. They were fun to tie, though. I started with yellow and orange feathers, and wound the thread around them. It was a great way to practice my knot-tying, which is something I do to keep from biting my fingernails. Also, the flies were kind of cute.

Jake and I took turns helping Nanny X paddle. We paused on the other side of the island, and she reached into the diaper bag and pulled out a bottle of baby powder. When she turned the end with the holes in it, no puffs of powder came out. Instead, the bottom of the bottle opened to reveal a lens. A baby-powder spyglass. She peered into the trees of Roosevelt Island. Then she passed the glass to me. It was crystal clear—not like regular binoculars, where you can never get the focus right. I didn't see anything suspicious, though.

The sky was brighter as we moved the canoe downstream toward the Tidal Basin and into deeper water. White clouds floated like marshmallows, toasted by the sun.

Nanny X took one of my flies, a blue one, and added it to her hat. It was like when my parents put one of my drawings on the refrigerator. Eliza sat on the bottom of the boat, babbling and scribbling in a coloring book.

"When I go fishing with Ethan," Jake said, "I catch something."

He had a point. I hadn't even seen many ripples in the water. Oh, the water moved, and you could see the current and feel it as it tugged our boat downstream. But those little ripples you're supposed to see when a fish comes up for air or a turtle ducks his head underwater? Nothing.

We spotted some boaters upstream and Nanny X held the spyglass to her sunglasses. I could tell even without the spyglass that they didn't look like the sort of people who had just threatened the president with a nine-foot fish sculpture. It made me wonder if the White House got other strange threats, like: *Sign this law or I'll hit you with a salami.*

Then I heard a *bloop*, like the sound the water drops make when the sink is leaking. I saw a ripple.

"There!" I pointed. "A fish."

"I don't see anything." Jake moved to the front of the boat, where Yeti was perched, and stood up to get a better view.

Yeti must have seen something in the water, too, because his nose was pointed right at the ripple.

The canoe rocked back and forth. Jake held up his fishing rod like he was on a tightrope and that was the pole he needed for balance.

Then the canoe hit a rush of water. We bounced, like we were going over a speed bump. The canoe turned sideways.

"*Weeeee,*" yelled Eliza.

My brother yelled, too. He dropped his fishing pole and tumbled over the side of the canoe, right into the Potomac.

"Jake!" My brother swims about as well as a copper sculpture of a fish. "Jake!"

Yeti jumped in after him, because he's pretty much the best dog in the world. But the current snatched them both, and they drifted down the middle of the river.

4. Jake

Nanny X Gets Some Help from a Purple Minnow

My friend Ethan has four survival guides, so when he got a fifth one he gave it to me. That's why I knew I wasn't drowning. The survival guide says that when people drown, they don't scream. I was screaming. *"Aaaaaaaaaahhhhhhhh."*

The second thing it says in the guide is that you should try not to panic. It was too late for that, so I skipped to step 3: Try to take in more air. You were supposed to be able to do this by floating on your back. The book forgets that floating on your back can be hard if you can't swim. But with the life jacket, floating was pretty easy. I tilted my head back, just like the book suggested. Slowly, my legs started to rise.

I could feel the cold water all around me. Slime and algae swirled around, too, like monster hair. I could feel wet dog. Plus, I could *smell* wet dog. When you are drowning, you do not pay attention to how things smell. Yeti paddled next to me. He licked some water off my nose.

"Hold on, Jake Z," called Nanny X.

"*I'm trying*," I yelled. But there was nothing for me to hold on to.

I felt something smooth and cold rub against my leg. My *Fantastically Freaky Animal Facts* book says all snakes can swim, including poisonous ones. What if I died from a snakebite instead of drowning?

"*Aaaahhhhhhhhh*," I yelled, a little higher.

"Can we help?" I whipped my head around and saw a small boat. Our friend Stinky, who is in fifth grade with Ali, was leaning over the side. The person steering was his nanny, Boris, who is a member of NAP, like Nanny X. They had their own fishing gear, which meant that they must be the special agents who got the case first. The good news was that they were in a perfect position to stop me before I drifted over a waterfall. Going over a waterfall is something that happens a lot in the movies.

"Aaaahh," I said, but not as loud.

Nanny X waved, like she was shooing them away. "We've got him covered." But she was nowhere near me. Then I saw her pluck a fishing lure from her hat and stick it in the water. It floated toward me, and grew from what looked like a purple minnow to a purple eggplant. It kept growing, until it was the size of a man-eating shark. But it wasn't eating anybody. What it was doing was swimming. What it was doing was coming to save me.

"Tundra," I said, which means that it was way cooler than just regular cool. After that, I stopped talking so water wouldn't get in my mouth.

The minnow reached me. Its tail was flat, like the bottom of a chair. There was a handle, and I grabbed it. My legs were still churning around in the water, so it took me a little while before I could pull myself up. I pulled Yeti up, too. He shook himself and I could see all kinds of ripples in the water where the drops fell. Slowly the minnow turned around and started swimming back toward Nanny X. *Upstream*. Which didn't seem possible. It had more control with its fins than Nanny X and my sister had with their paddles.

The minnow moved forward until it bumped smack into the canoe. Ali helped us on board, and Nanny X squeezed the minnow's cheeks so its fish lips looked even fishier. *Pppffffft*. It sounded like a whoopee cushion as it shrank back to its original size. Nanny X snatched it out of the water and stuck it back on her hat. Then she squeezed me.

"I guess I should start swimming lessons again," I said.

"It's not a bad skill for a special agent to have," she agreed, as Stinky and Boris buzzed toward us. Their boat had a motor. When they were a few feet away they cut it off, and Boris pulled out a hook—not for fishing, but for grabbing—and attached our boat to his. Then he pulled out a small anchor and threw it over the side.

"Fancy meeting you on this fine morning," said Boris, who is tall, even when he is sitting in a boat. He has brown skin and a little beard that Eliza likes to pull on.

"Hello, Boris," said Nanny X. She sounded kind of frosty. Not frosty as in cool or tundra; frosty as in angry.

"What have you caught?" he said.

"Not a person, place or thing," Nanny X admitted.

"We report the same," Boris said. Nanny X got a little friendlier after that.

"But *why* isn't anything out here?" Stinky asked. "That's just wrong." Stinky is very concerned about the environment. Not seeing any live fish probably bugged him a lot more than not seeing The Angler.

"Ali saw a ripple, before I fell in," I said. I thought that might cheer him up.

"It's true," Ali said. "Jake's splash scared whatever it was. But there was something out there."

"Dare. Dare!" Eliza pointed. We looked, but we didn't see anything. Eliza puffed up her cheeks and blew out a breath. If she were a grown-up, it would have been a sigh. Then she went back to her coloring book while Nanny X and Boris talked about which parts of the river they'd covered and wasn't it nice to be working together again? And did anyone happen to see a suspicious-looking character on shore with a sketchpad or maybe a blowtorch?

No one had.

Eliza ripped a page out of her coloring book.

"Eliza," Ali said. "That's not how we treat books."

Eliza held up a picture of a mouse wearing overalls and balled it up, like a baseball. She inherited that from me.

I looked at Stinky, who was talking about healthy rivers, and at Nanny X, who kept saying, "Yes, but what's the motive?"

"Fame?" said Boris.

"The Angler is anonymous," said Nanny X.

"The Angler is pseudonymous," said Boris. "A person can be known by a pseudonym. *You* are known by a pseudonym."

"Pseudonym," which is a name someone uses in place of their real name, would be a good reading-connection word, but I was too wet to write that one down.

"Maybe there's a political point," said Nanny X.

"Maybe the artist is making a statement that if we don't take better care of our rivers, the fish are going to end up on dry land," said Stinky.

"Actually," I told him, "some fish can survive on dry

land. Like mudskippers and the climbing gourami." I don't think you'd find a climbing gourami on the White House lawn, though; they live in Africa and parts of Asia.

"Pish!" said Eliza. She was holding my fishing pole.

"Eliza," Ali said, "be careful of the hook. It's sharp!"

"Sarp!" Eliza said. She took the hook and put her coloring-book paper on there. *Pppppping.* She dropped the line into the water.

Then, all of a sudden, the line went straight. I'd been fishing enough times with Ethan to know what that meant.

The flies hadn't worked. Neither had Weinrib's Canadian Night Crawlers. But somehow a piece of soggy coloring-book paper *had* worked. My baby sister had caught a fish.

5. Alison

Nanny X Reels One In

Eliza had no idea what to do with that fish. She didn't even realize she'd caught one. For all she knew, there was a sea monster on the end of that line. Or a cantaloupe. She puckered her lips and her eyebrows got all wavy as the fishing rod bent toward the water.

"Pull, Eliza," I said. "Pull it up."

But I guess all of that movement on the end of the line was too scary.

"Bad," Eliza said, as the end of the pole dipped down and the reel started spinning. Eliza threw the rod on the floor of the canoe.

Nanny X snatched it up and turned the handle. I suppose I should stop being surprised when Nanny X moves quickly. It's like a snake stalking a mouse: slow, slow, and then *bam*.

Jake leaned over the side of the canoe—hadn't he

learned his lesson?—and reported on her progress like a sports announcer.

"It's moving through the water. It's almost here. Closer. Closer. I can see it!"

And then so could we. Nanny X reached down and grabbed the line with her hand. She pulled a gleaming fish out of the water.

"Oh!" Eliza said.

The fish flicked its tail, and Yeti barked and sniffed it. Then he lost interest and went back to his end of the canoe.

"Good job, Eliza," I said. But Eliza lost interest, just like Yeti. She started coloring again.

The fish was smaller than you would have thought for all of that pulling—about the size of Boris's right hand, which was reaching out toward the fish, holding a pair of scissors to cut the line.

When he did, Nanny X put the fish in a white bucket, and we peered inside.

The fish was slightly reddish in color, with a lower lip that stuck out, like it was pouting. Its body was shaped like the leaves on the rhododendron my dad planted last fall.

"It looks sick," said Stinky.

"That's how I'd look if I were caught." I made my eyes sort of sad and googly, to show him.

"He's a strange color," Stinky said.

"But the tail's moving in a healthy way," I said. Still, two other things bothered me.

One: The fish had gills, but the gills *weren't* moving, which meant it wasn't breathing, right?

And two: We weren't supposed to be obsessing over the health of the fish or even the river. We were supposed to be fishing for a *criminal*—a criminal who had threatened the president of the United States. A criminal who had threatened to destroy national treasures starting at noon, which was only two hours away. Time was running out.

"This fish," Nanny X announced, "is a Pacific herring." How could NAP think she didn't know enough about fish to take the case?

Jake looked confused. "There shouldn't be any Pacific herring in the Potomac," he said. Jake reads a lot of books that have animal facts, but this bit of knowledge didn't come from a book; it came from the Fish of the Potomac place mat he'd bought at the hardware store. Only my brother would spend his allowance on a place mat. "Bass," Jake recited. "Perch. Pickerel. Black drum. Plus, Pacific herring are found in the *Pacific*."

"Maybe it got here accidentally," Stinky said. "Maybe they stocked the river with Pacific herring for a fishing tournament, which would be irresponsible to the ecosystem."

Nanny X lifted the fish by the snippet of fishing line. "It's heavy. Heavier than it should be. Still, I wonder if it would work for lunch."

Leave it to Nanny X to find a way to cook a fish in a canoe in the middle of the river. My stomach got queasy as Nanny X took the fish in her hands and turned it over.

"That's odd," she said. She reached into her diaper bag and pulled out a pair of baby nail clippers. She pushed a button, and out came a sharp knife that shouldn't be anywhere near a baby. Eliza looked up, and she was *mad*. Even if she wasn't interested in the fish, that didn't mean she wanted Nanny X doing anything to it.

"Distract her," Nanny X said to me.

Wait a minute, I thought. *What kind of nanny kills a fish in front of an almost-two-year-old? Or an almost-eleven-year-old?*

"I don't believe it's even alive," Nanny X said, reading my mind again.

"But the tail is moving."

"True." But Nanny X didn't put her knife away. She waited until Eliza turned to look at a butterfly that landed on the side of the canoe. Then she plunged the knife into the fish, just behind the dorsal fin. There was a crunching sound as she cut a small slit in the fish's back.

I expected Nanny X's hand to fill up with blood and fish guts. But there was no blood. She tilted the fish upside down and her hand filled with a bunch of cogs and gears.

"Just as I thought," she said.

Boris pulled a small bag out of his pocket (his pants had an awful lot of pockets) and held it beneath the fish, so that none of the parts got away.

Nanny X held up the bag to show Eliza. "Broken," she told her. "Toy."

But it wasn't exactly a toy. And it wasn't exactly a fish, either. It was a robot.

6. Jake

Nanny X Gets Held Up by a Squirrel

We unhooked the boats and started moving. Nanny X took us under a bridge and into the Tidal Basin, where the current wouldn't flop us around anymore. We saw the white dome of the Jefferson Memorial, and lots and lots of people.

"Something's fishy," said Nanny X.

I thought it was weird that the thing that made Eliza's fish *less* fishy (meaning gears and things) actually made it *more* fishy (meaning suspicious).

"We've got mysteries out the ying-yang," Nanny X said. "Who can tell me what they are?"

"Someone named The Angler is trying to force the president to put a fish statue on the White House lawn," Ali said. "And we don't know why."

"We caught a robot fish," I added. "And we don't know why."

Maybe those things weren't connected. But one weird fish thing plus another weird fish thing happening on the same day seemed like more than a coincidence. Of course, with Nanny X, there were always weird fish things. I was just glad that this weird fish thing didn't involve my lunch.

Now that it was warmer, people were renting paddle-boats—the kind you pedal, like a bicycle—so we weren't the only ones on the water. Nanny X scanned the crowd again with her spyglass. I hoped my new powers of observation would catch something that everyone else missed, but nobody looked suspicious or artsy. Nothing looked out of the ordinary, except for the robot fish.

Nanny X looked at her watch. "Ninety minutes," she said. "I have one more thought as to where The Angler could be killing time." She pointed to another bridge across the basin, and the passageway beneath it. "That leads to the waterfront. And you know what's there."

"The baseball stadium!" I said.

"The fish market!" said Ali. We'd visited the Nationals' stadium more than we'd visited the fish market, which was where we got oysters the one day a year our mom made oyster stew. I had a feeling we'd be visiting the fish market a lot more with Nanny X around.

"Brilliant," Boris said. "I'll give you a tow."

Nanny X didn't look like she wanted any help, but my arms felt all noodle-y from paddling. If this kept up, I wouldn't even be able to swing a bat at my baseball game against the Green Sox. If we were done being special agents in time to even *go* to my game, which was at six o'clock on the nose, as Nanny X would say.

"A tow would be arctic!" I told Boris.

But Nanny X did something even more arctic: She took another fishing lure from her hat and attached it to the back of our canoe. *Bbbbbbbbbbbbrrrrrttt.* It might have been the world's tiniest motor, but it zipped us across the water ahead of Boris and Stinky, who started their own motor and followed us. Our boats left a wake, which blurped some of the paddleboaters around. They looked angry, but I don't think they were angry at us; mostly, I think, they were tired of pedaling.

"Government business," Nanny X told them. She stood with one foot on the side of the boat and dipped her paddle in the water to help control our direction. She looked like that picture of George Washington crossing the Delaware, except Washington wore a different kind of hat.

We went through a tunnel under a bridge and pulled into a small marina, which is a parking lot for boats. There was even a spot with our name on it: NAP. Both boats fit in there, side by side. I helped tie the canoe to a post. Then we pulled out the stroller, the diaper bag, the coloring book and the bag with the mechanical fish parts, and went to explore the market.

It smelled worse than my lunch box the day Nanny X gave me the anchovy sandwich. But there were good smells, too; they were just hiding underneath the bad ones.

We walked by stalls with piles of scallops and shrimp and crabs and fish. Lots and lots of fish. They were the whole kind, with their heads still on and their mouths wide open. Ali was as googly-eyed as the fish were. I think the smell was getting to her.

"Our scallops pack a wallop," said the man behind the counter of Fernando's Fish Hut. He smiled like on a TV commercial, where people act very excited about insurance or Doritos or cars. "Our grouper is super. Our crab is fab."

A lady walked up and took a photo of him standing behind the seafood. He kept smiling for the photo, but then he stopped smiling and shook his head.

"All people do is take pictures. Yesterday somebody stood here and actually drew one of my catfish."

Drew? That could be a clue. "What did he look like?" I asked.

"Oh, about yay big and kind of slimy. He had a mustache like my Uncle Dusty."

"Sorry, I didn't mean the catfish," I said politely. "I meant what did the person *drawing* the catfish look like?"

"Hard to tell. He had a hat pulled down and he wore a rain slicker. I tried to sell him my scallops but all he cared about was that fish. I wish he'd cared enough to buy it."

I think he knew that I was not going to buy a catfish, either. But then Nanny X came up and bought six bowls of Fernando's Couldn't-Be-Prouder Clam Chowder, which made him happy. There were saltine crackers, too. We ate them outside in this porch-y area that had tables but no chairs. Stinky ate his chowder, after going back to tell Fernando that it would be better for the environment if he didn't serve the chowder in Styrofoam.

Boris ate, too, after saying what a shame it was that no one at the fish market sold lentil soup. (Boris liked lentils the way Nanny X liked fish.) He poured the bag of robot fish parts on the table.

"Look at the craftsmanship here, in the mouth," he said. The fish had tiny spiky teeth, the size of lettuce seeds. Chunks of Eliza's coloring-book page were still stuck between them.

Nanny X brushed away some cracker crumbs and pulled out a thin package of baby wipes. The soapy smell didn't fool me. The mini baby wipes package was really her NAP computer, which gave us direct access to 149 different crime databases.

She clicked on a couple of keys.

"Type in 'paper,'" Boris suggested. "And 'herring.' Is there anything for 'paper-eating herring'?"

"I know what to type, thanks," said Nanny X. *Click, click, click* went the keys. "Nothing."

"Robot fish?" I suggested.

Click, click.

"No."

Some seagulls came over to see if we had any more crackers, but we didn't.

Then we heard a sound that was a cross between clicking and gargling. It didn't come from the seagulls or Yeti or from Nanny X's computer, either. The sound came from a squirrel. He was the darkest brown, with a fluffy tail and shining eyes. He looked a little sad. He ran up to Nanny X, who kept typing.

"I'm sorry," Boris told the squirrel. "We don't have any food for you."

The squirrel scooted closer anyway. He climbed onto the table. His tail flicked up and down and he made that click-gargle sound again.

That's when he opened his mouth. He grabbed Nanny X's computer with his teeth, which were much bigger than the fish's.

"Holy cats!" Nanny X said, even though it was a squirrel. He ran down the table and jumped off the end, heading through the market. Then he crossed a busy street and started running up the grassy hill on the other side.

Nanny X moved fast, but she did not move as fast as that squirrel. By the time we'd zigagged through the market and crossed the street, we could make out the squirrel climbing a tree in the distance. We caught up to him and then *spro-*

ing. He jumped to the next tree. We followed the sound of rattling leaves.

"I can't let that computer get into the wrong hands," Nanny X said. "NAP would be...disappointed."

I didn't point out that squirrels had paws instead of hands, because actually? They look like hands. Here are some other things I know about squirrels, thanks to my *Fantastically Freaky* book.

One: Their front teeth grow forever, so they have to chew on things like walnuts to keep their teeth short. The book doesn't mention chewing on computers.

Two: People have used squirrels as spies.

Nanny X must have read that book, too; that's why she was so worried. Because if this squirrel was being used for spying, he could be taking Nanny X's computer to the enemy.

Fortunately we had Yeti, who is a professional squirrel chaser. At home, all you have to do is say "Squirrel!" and he will run straight to our bird feeder, where there are always squirrels trying to steal birdseed.

But Yeti didn't run. He sniffed the air and then walked over to Boris and sniffed his shoes.

"Squirrel!" I said again. Yeti looked at me like I was talking in pig latin.

The squirrel moved to a tree where the branches were low enough for me to grab. But as soon as I started climbing, the squirrel changed trees.

We needed someone who could move quicker than we could, someone who was extremely flexible and who was on our side. It would help if he was furry and could move from tree to tree like that squirrel.

"We need Howard," I said.

7. Alison

Nanny X Grabs the Remote

Squirrel spies? Seriously?

I'd heard plenty of crazy things since Nanny X started taking care of us. And those things turned out to be true. But a squirrel guilty of espionage? Besides, we were supposed to be looking for fish, and for someone who liked fish enough to sculpt them. We didn't have time for squirrels. But I knew we had to get Nanny X's computer back, especially if NAP had any doubts about her skills as a special agent. She had something to prove. All of us did. And enlisting Howard actually seemed like a decent idea.

I should probably explain that Howard is a chimp. He helped us solve our last case. Jake got kind of attached to him, but we weren't allowed to bring him home because A, we had Yeti, and B, Nanny X said chimps were meant to live in the wild. As a compromise, Howard went to live at the David T. Jones Primate Sanctuary.

"Can we get him here quickly?" Boris asked.

"Transportation can be arranged," Nanny X said. She reached into the diaper bag and pulled out a diaper.

"*Aha!*" yelled Jake. He'd yelled that almost every time Nanny X pulled out a diaper this week, thinking it was going to be a new diaper phone, but every time it was a regular diaper. This time she opened it up to reveal three rows of silver buttons. She dialed.

"X here," she said. "Permission to use Operation Baseball."

Jake's ears pricked up when she said "baseball."

"Right," she said. "It's the most efficient way. X out."

She had started to dial again when Jake yelled, "*Squirrel on the move!*"

The tree rattled and the squirrel came down the trunk and started running, with Jake right behind him. Stinky and Boris started running, too, but I wasn't sure if they were keeping track of the squirrel or keeping track of Jake.

I got stuck playing with Eliza near a cement circle by a sign that said L'Enfant Plaza while Nanny X talked to the primate sanctuary.

There was some concern at the other end of the phone, I could tell. Nanny X tried out a bunch of words like "government request," "service to country," "patriotism," "important," "matter of national security," "hero chimpanzees." She used another word, too: "please." That one seemed to work.

"Oh, you see it now? Wonderful. Yes. It's perfectly safe. Don't forget the seat belt."

A moment later she folded up the diaper and put it back in the bag.

"So how is Howard getting here?" I asked Nanny X.

"He's flying."

Nanny X pulled out a toy radio—the wind-up kind

with pictures on it. Usually the pictures are of a cow jumping over the moon, but on this one there was a picture of a spaceship. Nanny X turned the knob. Then she opened the back to reveal a control panel. She punched in a few numbers.

"Nanny X?" I said.

"Our coordinates," she explained. "He'll be here soon."

Meanwhile Jake, Boris and Stinky had disappeared down the hill. They must have followed the squirrel between some buildings. I paced around the cement circle with Eliza and Yeti. Nanny X paced with us.

After about ten minutes she gave us the countdown: five, four, three, two, one. We heard a whirring sound. "Ah," said Nanny X as something that looked like a yellow crab with propellers on it appeared overhead. Its legs clutched a large, white ball that was way bigger than a baseball.

The flying crab thing was a drone. I'd seen an article about drones in the paper, when a company used one to deliver a pizza. But the white ball was way bigger than a pizza, too. I hoped it had lots of padding, because the pizza had ended up splatted in the middle of the Capital Beltway.

When the drone reached the ground, the legs released the ball, which was about the size of a Hippity Hop, and landed beside it. The ball rolled back and forth for a second before stopping. A panel opened. Nanny X reached inside and clicked a seat belt that was restraining something brown and furry.

"Eeeee, eeee," said Howard. He was wearing a crash helmet, but as soon as Nanny X helped him take it off, he put on her old gardening hat, which he was holding carefully in two hairy hands.

"Very fashionable," said Nanny X. She handed him a

banana from the diaper bag. There were at least a dozen more in there.

I reached out my own not-hairy hand to shake Howard's. But the chimp lifted his arms, the way Eliza does when she says "Up, up." I lifted him and he gave me a big, wet chimpanzee kiss, right on the mouth. Yeti jumped up on both of us. I'm pretty sure he was just saying hello.

Just then, a couple of tourists wandered up the hill to take in the view of the river below. But none of them even glanced at the river. They were all staring at us. Nanny X punched in some more coordinates and the drone lifted off again. While the tourists looked up to watch it, Nanny X grabbed the stroller and Eliza. I offered Howard a piggyback ride, and we went down the hill in search of Jake.

If we found him, we'd find that stupid squirrel. And if we could find the squirrel, we could get on to our real assignment, which was finding The Angler before something besides Nanny X's computer disappeared. I had another assignment, too, but that one wasn't official: solving the case before Stinky and Boris did, so NAP would know the Pringles were meant to be special agents. And then they'd know our nanny was meant to be one, too.

8. Jake

Nanny X Gets Some Help from a Chimp

Squirrels can run twenty miles per hour.

Humans can run twenty-seven miles per hour, but only if they are Usain Bolt. We had an advantage, because we weren't running around with computers in our mouths. But the squirrel could climb. He went up trees, and down them. He went up buildings and onto ledges.

We split up, with Boris on one side of a building, me in the middle and Stinky on the end. We looked like a SWAT team, except that we didn't have black T-shirts and we didn't have guns and one of us had really soggy shoes from falling into the Potomac River.

Boris pulled something from one of his pockets. He didn't carry nearly as much as Nanny X did, maybe because Stinky didn't wear diapers. But he had a hook. I wasn't just a fish hook, either. It was a small grappling hook, like the one he'd used to hold our boats together, with a rope hanging from it like a tail. He attached it to a tree and tried to swing it toward the next tree after the squirrel. The squirrel was too fast; I almost expected him to stick out his tongue at us.

"Okay, then," said Boris. He pulled out a small green disc and sent it whizzing through the air. It opened into a net, and caught a fire hydrant.

The squirrel went back to the sidewalk and ran jerkily down the hill again.

We heard footsteps as Ali and Nanny X and Eliza caught up with us. Ali had someone on her back, and it didn't take me long to figure out that the someone was Howard!

He jumped down and hugged me around the legs. I guess he'd missed me, too.

"You should have seen it," said Ali. "He came in a drone."

It wasn't surprising that NAP owned a drone. Plus, it made sense that they used it for Howard. Chimps and monkeys have a proven record of being excellent fliers. They were sent into space before humans.

"Where's our squirrel friend?" asked Nanny X.

"Up there." Boris pointed to a tree that was growing out of a space in the sidewalk.

Nanny X made a sign with both of her pointer fingers, like she was doing some sort of boogie-woogie dance. Then she held up a package of baby wipes—real ones. Howard took off his gardening hat and handed it to Nanny X like he understood her sign language perfectly. He went to the tree and started to climb. When he reached a high branch, he swung for a minute like he was hanging from a trapeze. Then he disappeared into the leaves. We heard a rattling sound as the squirrel moved to the next tree, but Howard was right behind him. They made a bunch of noise, like they were arguing with their mouths full of Listerine.

"Eeeeeee," Howard said, getting in the last word. He

climbed down the tree, one-handed. In his other hand he carried Nanny X's baby-wipe computer.

"Good work, Howard!" said Nanny X, handing him a banana.

You too, Jake, I thought to myself. Because I was the one who thought of calling Howard in the first place. Though I guess a diaper bag full of bananas meant that Nanny X might have planned on calling him, too. What I said out loud was: "There is something weird about that squirrel."

"You think?" said Ali. This is called sarcasm. Because duh, there were lots of weird things about that squirrel.

"Did you notice the way it moved?" I said. "It didn't move like normal squirrels do."

In real life, squirrels have ankles that rotate. That's why they don't come down trees backward, the way humans and chimps do; they come running down headfirst.

But *this* squirrel came down in reverse. Plus, it didn't have the smooth, hoppy motion most squirrels have.

"Yeti didn't do his squirrel trick, either," I said. At first I'd thought that meant something was wrong with Yeti. Now I thought it meant there was something wrong with the squirrel. "We should keep following him," I added. "He's suspicious."

We were close to the bottom of the hill now. We were also close to people, and they seemed to be looking at us— at Howard, especially.

Eliza took off her sun bonnet and waved it around.

"Eliza, that's a great idea," I said.

We pulled some extra stuff out of Nanny X's diaper bag. Soon Howard was wearing Eliza's bonnet, an extra pair of her overalls and a pink shirt. I pointed to the stroller.

"Go ahead, Howard," I said. "Get in." Howard squeezed into the stroller next to Eliza. Nanny X pulled down the sun visor, and from a distance you couldn't tell my sister's seat-mate was a chimpanzee. The squirrel came down the tree and ran the rest of the way down the hill, toward the Smithsonian Castle.

"That's where my art exhibit is," said Ali. But the squirrel switched directions again and turned right, toward the Hirshhorn Museum.

We followed him, past an ice-cream truck and about a bazillion people. Then the squirrel crossed another street and disappeared into the Hirshhorn's outdoor sculpture garden.

Ali and I have spent a lot of time at the sculpture garden. We like to play hide-and-seek there, even though it's supposed to be a spot for "quiet contemplation." The squirrel was playing hide-and-seek now.

"Squirrel, Yeti," I said. But he just looked in the stroller at Howard. Howard looked back like he was thinking *Now what?*

That's what I wanted to know, too.

9. Alison

Nanny X Takes a Nap

I was happy about three things.

One: I didn't have wet feet, like Jake.

Two: We were away from the water and officially on land in Washington, D.C., where we could get down to the business of catching The Angler and maybe, eventually, go see my painting.

Three: The sculpture garden seemed like the perfect place to solve a mystery about someone who wanted to put a sculpture on the White House lawn. It was one of my favorite places on the whole Mall. I liked it because instead of going inside a quiet museum to look at strange art, you could stay outside in the sunshine and look at it.

And it looked like the strange art was about to get a little stranger.

"I am not an art expert," Boris said, "but I think *The Great Warrior of Montauban* has a problem with his hand."

The Warrior of Montauban had problems with other

body parts, too. He was missing his knees and the bottom parts of his legs. He was also missing pants. And a shirt.

He had a sword, though, a big one behind his back. And he had very muscular arms. One of his arms extended out to the side, and at the end of that arm was a giant hand. But his thumb was hanging from his hand at an odd angle.

"Maybe it's getting rusty," said Jake.

Nanny X squatted down beneath the arm and looked up at the thumb to get a closer look.

"Watch out!" I said.

The thumb waved a little, like it was barely even attached. Then it plunked like a raindrop, straight onto Nanny X's head. Our nanny swayed back and forth as the thumb thumped onto the grass. Boris caught her before she joined it. He set her down, gently. When he removed her mirrored sunglasses, her eyes were closed. "She's unconscious," he said. He slid the thumb, which looked like it weighed about fifty pounds, into an evidence bag.

"Nanny X, wake up!" I said. I wondered what NAP would do about an agent who lost a computer and got knocked out on the same mission. I fanned her with my hands, because sometimes air revives people when they are unconscious. Soon our nanny's eyes fluttered. When she opened them, the first thing she did was look at her watch. I thought it was because she was trying to figure out how long she'd been knocked out, but I was wrong. "It's almost noon," she said. "The thumb is a warning."

She didn't say who was warning us, but we knew: The Angler.

We tried to help Nanny X over to a bench.

"I am not a frail old lady," she said. "I'm very spry." She plopped down on the bench, reached into the diaper bag and grabbed Mr. Ow, a cold pack in the shape of an octopus that Eliza uses when she gets a bad bump. Nanny X took off her fishing hat, put Mr. Ow on her head and set the fishing hat back in place. Then she opened up her mini computer.

The screen was blue. The computer made a sound, sort of like *Moo, Sweet Cow*, only it sounded a little more like *Moo*, Sick *Cow*. Nanny X slammed the computer shut again.

"We're running out of time," I said, which didn't help.

"Indeed," said Boris, dropping Montauban's thumb into the diaper bag. "We will have to choose our plan carefully."

While Boris and Nanny X talked about their strategy, I walked over to the Yoko Ono Wishing Tree, the spot in the sculpture garden where people write down wishes and hang them from the branches.

A lot of the wishes were for world peace. One said, "I wish for a million dollars." One said, "I wish my mom would get better."

I took a pencil and wrote on a slip of paper: "I wish we could catch The Angler." I wrote "we." I meant "I." But I knew it was going to take more than wishes to solve our case.

I found a low branch and was hanging up my wish when I noticed another wish, in swirly, slanted handwriting. "I wish the president would get some new art for his front lawn," it said. On the back of the paper it had one word: "Mine."

I guess there could be a lot of people who wanted their art to be discovered. But there were not a lot of people who said out loud that they wanted their art to be on the front lawn of the White House. I looked at the swirly handwriting again. It had an artistic quality to it. It also looked like a woman's handwriting. I don't know why we all automatically thought we were searching for a bad *guy*. Maybe The Angler was a woman.

"*Hey,*" I yelled.

"Hay is for horses," said Nanny X. That meant that she was feeling a little better. She came over to see.

Except for the "mine," the white tag was unsigned, like all of the other wishes.

"It's a clue," I said. "The Angler was *just here*."

"Wait a minute, now," Boris said. "How often do they collect these wishes? I'm not saying it's not The Angler, but this wish could have been hanging on the tree for a very long time."

"I know how to find out," I said. I ran up the steps of the garden, two at a time. Stinky followed me, even though I could have done it alone. I guess he felt that as a safety patrol, it was one of his responsibilities to see that I got across the street safely.

"Where are you going?" he asked.

"To ask a question about my clue." I used "my" just to remind him that whatever answer I got was mine, too. If I couldn't solve the mystery first, I wanted to solve it the best.

I spotted a security guard near the fountain and ran straight up to her.

"What happens to the wishes on the Yoko Tree?" I said it really fast, Nanny X style.

"Well, they're harvested," she said. "Like apples. And sent to Iceland, to the Yoko Ono Peace Tower."

"How often do you harvest them?" That was the important part.

"Every day."

That meant the wish had to have been written *in the last twenty-four hours*. The Angler was close.

"*Thank you*," I shouted, and ran back to the others, with Stinky looking both ways as we crossed the street. Nanny X snapped a photo of the wish with her diaper phone, and

Boris used his modified iPod to scan the wish for finger-prints. Stinky said it played "Secret Agent Man" whenever he did that, but we couldn't hear it without the ear buds. If I solved the case, I would write a song called "Secret Agent Woman."

Boris put the iPod away and started punching words into his phone. "Fish." "President." "Sculpture." It may not have been connected to the same crime databases as Nanny X's computer, but a whole bunch of stories came up. There was one about a sculpture of a hogfish that had been given to President Kennedy by the president of Bermuda.

There were stories that didn't have anything to do with presidents, fish or sculptures. And then there was this story in *Artsy Bartsy* magazine: "Fish Art Overstays Welcome."

The story was a review of a show by an artist named Ursula (no last name) that was appearing at a Georgetown gallery. Apparently most of her artwork had to do with fish.

"I am trying to capture the beauty of the ocean before it is destroyed by global warming," she said, which made Stinky like her right off. But the magazine's reviewer, a guy named Bartholomew Huffleberger, didn't like her one bit.

"The problem with fish," he wrote, "is that they stink after a relatively short time. We would be better off if this exhibit closed immediately."

10. Jake

Nanny X Heads for the White House

My homework for Monday was as good as done, because that art review had more reading-connection words than I've ever found in one place. It started like this:

An artist known by the moniker of Ursula opened her one-woman show at Gallery 24 in Georgetown last night, and I, for one, would have been in a more convivial mood had I been attending a closing instead. Ursula's work is didactic, shows no innovation, and is redundant besides. Her inspiration is the fish, and like the creature she so admires, I find her work malodorous. Her paintings appear realistic enough, but her fishes' sad eyes give them the twee appearance of Precious Moments figurines. Like Ursula's much-loved salmon, the artist will have to fight her way upstream. This reviewer was not hooked, and when he told the artist of his disappointment, she smeared his suit with salmon pâté.

Nanny X explained some of the words: "didactic" (which means you're being too lecture-y), "convivial" (which means pleasant and agreeable), "pâté" (which means ground-up meat or fish) and "moniker" (which I already figured out meant name). The part I didn't have to ask about came in the last paragraph, when he said that one of Ursula's fish sculptures looked like a turnip and she should go back to doing arts and crafts with the local Girl Scout troop. Plus, he said that the gallery should have installed a show by his eight-year-old niece instead.

Boris punched more words into his phone—"Ursula," "fish" and "art"—so we could find a picture of her work. All he got was a bunch of pictures of the Sea Witch from *The Little Mermaid*.

But he also saw a breaking news story about the art world. Portrait of President Washington Disappears from National Gallery of Art," the headline said.

Nanny X looked at her watch again. "Ten past noon," she said. "This is it. The Angler has made the first move."

Ali stared at the ground and looked like she'd been the one who was hit in the head with a giant thumb. It was a full minute before any of us said anything.

"A portrait of George Washington doesn't seem like much of a treasure," I said, to make everybody feel better. "As long as it wasn't the one of him crossing the Delaware. There are loads of portraits of Washington. Aren't there?"

Boris shook his head. "It says here that this was a rare portrait painted by the artist Salvador Dali. He did not live in Washington's time, of course, but he's very famous. Nobody knew the portrait existed until three months ago when it was discovered at a flea market. This article even hails it as 'a new national treasure.' It's worth millions.'"

I thought we would go straight to the gallery until Ali said, "We should go see Bartholomew Huffleberger. I'll bet he could give us a list of people who could have made the fish statue. He could tell us if one of them was Ursula."

"How can he do that if he's never seen the fish statue?" I said. "*We* haven't even seen it." I looked at Nanny X. "Do we have a picture?"

Nanny X lifted her hat. She took Mr. Ow off her head and put it back in the diaper bag. "I checked on that last night," she said. "The statue was in transit to the White House. No photo was available."

"I checked this morning," Boris said, "and was told the same thing. But surely the statue must be there by now."

"Then we should go see it," Stinky said.

"Museum," I said.

"Reviewer," said Ali.

"We are a big team, no?" said Boris. "Perhaps we need to divide and conquer once more. I will take Ali to see this *Artsy Bartsy.*"

"I'll take Jake to the White House and get a visual," said Nanny X. "We'll meet at the National Gallery."

Of course they were doing my idea last. I pretended that was because it was the best, like when you're the cleanup batter in baseball. "Howard gets to come with us, though, right?" I said.

"Right."

"We get Yeti," said Ali.

"And me," added Stinky. He turned a little reddish, probably because he'd just said we should be going to the White House. Or maybe because he liked my sister. It is amazing the things you can notice when you are working on your powers of observation. I was ready for action, even if my shoes were still squishy.

Nanny X called the White House to let them know we were coming. Her diaper phone has a direct line there.

"You're sure you're okay?" Boris asked Nanny X.

"Fine," she said, touching her hat.

"Okay, then." Boris took off with my sister and Stinky. Nanny X reached into her diaper bag and pulled out her bunny slippers. At first I thought she was going to give them to me instead of my squishy shoes. But she took off her own shoes and slid them on. Then she whistled. A pedicab driver came biking toward us, pulling a chair like a chariot.

"Get in," said Nanny X. "You too, Howard."

Howard adjusted his bonnet and climbed from the stroller into the pedicab. "Sixteen hundred Pennsylvania Avenue," Nanny X told the driver.

"The White House?"

"Precisely."

"What about you and Eliza?" I said. Nanny X had just gotten conked on the head. She needed to sit down. But the pedicab would be a little crowded with four of us, plus Eliza's stroller.

"Don't worry about me," said Nanny X. She reached into the bag and pulled out an old-fashioned motorcycle helmet, the leather kind that matched her motorcycle jacket. Then she pushed the noses on her bunny slippers. Wheels popped out of the bottoms. She looked pretty spry as she skated over to the bike path, pushing Eliza in the stroller.

I leaned over to Howard. "She's being conspicuous again," I said. "Very conspicuous."

At least no one was looking at him anymore; they were looking at our nanny, who was skating expertly down Independence Avenue.

Howard and I settled back as our driver pedaled past a bus. He signaled right and turned onto Fourteenth Street. Howard signaled, too, like he knew just what it meant. He gave me a thumbs-up as the driver put on the brakes, right in front of the White House gate.

11. Alison

Nanny X Is Out of the Picture

I was running ahead of Stinky even though he had longer legs and even though it wasn't supposed to be a race. Sometimes it felt like the only thing I was the best at was biting my fingernails. I wanted to be the best at something real and important, like solving our case so we could keep our jobs. Being faster than Stinky made me feel better.

But when I looked back over my shoulder and saw our nanny roller-skating in a blur of pink bunny slippers, I stopped running and started laughing.

"Are those bunny slippers?" Boris asked as Nanny X passed a line of people riding on Segways, which look like dollies, the kind the UPS man uses for moving heavy packages.

I nodded.

"State of the art!" he said. "This is the first time I've seen them in action." I could tell he was wishing for bunny slippers, too. But he'd been assigned the case first. Maybe he didn't need bunny slippers to get ahead.

"Why didn't the Secret Service just release a photo of the fish statue when they got the threat?" I asked. "It should have been in the news."

"That is exactly what The Angler wanted," Boris said. "Publicity."

Stinky added: "If The Angler's fish was on the front page of the paper, everyone would be sending statues to the president."

We started running again, a gentle jog this time, not a race (except that I was still in the lead). Soon we reached the *Artsy Bartsy* office.

I imagined Jake knocking on the door of the White House, but I wasn't jealous; I'd been on a field trip there just before Christmas. Ms. Bertram had spent half the time yelling at us because we'd tried to whistle for the president's dog.

I knocked on *Artsy Bartsy's* blue door. I was still knocking when I heard an "Ahem" behind me. It came from a tall man with black hair that stood up a little. He wore the tweedy jacket professors wear when they want to look like professors. He also had small, rectangular glasses, which were perched on a nose that was longish and kind of skinny.

"Were you looking for me?"

"Are you Bartholomew Huffleberger?" asked Boris.

"I am."

"We'd like to ask some questions about an art exhibit you reviewed six months ago."

"Which one?" the critic said.

"It featured an artist named Ursula."

His skinny nose wrinkled.

"Was her show really that bad?" asked Boris.

"It depends on what you mean by 'bad,'" said the critic. "Did it make a statement? Perhaps. But what a disaster. It was as if she'd thrown her entire wardrobe of clothing onto the floor and said, 'There. How do I look?' Some of the pieces were okay, but was it groundbreaking? No. Was it truly art?"

"I thought everything counted as art," said Stinky. Our art teacher, Mrs. Bonawali, told us that even a can of soup could be art.

"The woman paints realistic fish with sad eyes," Mr. Huffleberger said. "Excuse me while I faint from excitement."

"Your review mentioned a sculpture," I said.

"She created some sculptures, yes. So does a child with a can of Play-Doh. I saw Ursula's work once long ago at a county fair. Believe me, she hasn't improved."

"Do you have any photographs of the artist's work?" Boris asked. "We're trying to see if there's a link between her and a certain sculpture we're researching." He didn't mention the president.

"Is this a school project?" Mr. Huffleberger looked at me and Stinky. "No matter. I have one photo here." He pulled out his phone and scrolled through until he found a photo of a painting of a sad-eyed fish. It looked pretty good from a distance.

"I noticed her website disappeared not long after my review," Mr. Huffleberger continued. "But I have her original publicity prints inside, if you'd like to take a look." He glanced at Yeti. "Wait here. I am a cat person."

He unlocked his office door and made a gasping sound. The room was as neat as Mr. Huffleberger himself. But the desk looked like someone had emptied a recycling bin on top of it. There were papers everywhere, with bite-sized chunks taken out of them.

"What's this?" said Mr. Huffleberger. "Picasso? Picasso, where are you?" I thought maybe Mr. Huffleberger had a Picasso painting hanging on his wall, which would count as a national treasure, and that someone—The Angler, for instance—had stolen it. But he rushed behind his desk and bear-hugged the world's largest cat, who was puffed up like a balloon at the Thanksgiving parade. Mr. Huffleberger looked through the door at us. "Who did you say you were?"

"Investigators," said Boris.

"Then investigate!"

I tied Yeti's leash around the lamppost and Stinky and I followed Boris into Mr. Huffleberger's office. Aside from the desk, everything was in its place. There was a lamp with a green shade and a coatrack with no coats. On the wall there was only one painting, and it wasn't by Picasso. The picture was of a moose. In the corner it said "Huffleberger."

"You paint?" Boris asked, as Mr. Huffleberger inspected the cat to make sure he hadn't been injured.

Mr. Huffleberger smiled a thin-lipped smile. "I used to," he said. "But I learned that my true calling is words."

I wondered what my true calling was. I didn't think it was math, even if I did get problem No. 7 right. Art was still a possibility. And special-agent work, as long as we didn't mess up this case.

Boris pulled up an antenna on the side of his iPod and used it to measure the bites on Mr. Huffleberger's papers. He was about to measure the bite of Mr. Huffleberger's cat, too, but Picasso let out a vampire hiss.

"I'll estimate," Boris said.

Mr. Huffleberger put his fingers on his neck, as if he was checking his pulse. "Who would do this to me?" he said. Something told me that a lot of people wanted to harm Mr. Huffleberger, including Ursula.

"About those photos..." I said, getting back to the original subject. A good special agent has to stay on task.

"If we must," he said. He put down the cat and opened the desk drawer to reveal a bunch of yellow folders. But under U, the only files he had were for "Umbrellas," "University" and "Untitled." The file for the artist named Ursula was missing.

12. Jake

Nanny X Reads Some Poetry

Nanny X changed from her bunny slippers to her regular shoes before we went into the White House. Then she led us past the people who were waiting in line for the one o'clock tour.

"May I help you?" asked the guard.

"Nanny X," said Nanny X. "We're with NAP." She waved her hands around to show that "we" meant me, too.

I expected the man to send us back to the end of the line. I expected him to say "Come back later." Instead he said, "We've been expecting you." He spoke into his walkie-talkie: "It's NAP."

"I'll be right out," a voice crackled back. A few minutes later someone came to meet us. She was not the president. She had short hair and wore a green dress and she walked almost as fast as Nanny X. She shined a blue light on Nanny X's badge. Then Nanny X pulled out IDs for me and Eliza and Howard. The woman looked at Howard's ID and then lifted back his bonnet so she could make sure his face matched his picture.

"Last week we had a visit from a sloth," said the woman, whose name tag said Camila Lopez. "This way." She led us away from the tourists to a private metal detector and sent us through, one by one. *Beeeeeeeeep.* The fishhooks on Nanny X's hat set off the metal detector. Ms. Lopez put the hat on a conveyor belt with Eliza's stroller and the diaper bag.

"NAP agent or not," she said, lifting the diaper bag and the stroller off the belt again, "these things stay here." Nanny X got to keep her hat, though.

Ms. Lopez opened a heavy wooden door, and we followed her into the main building. "Welcome to the White House," she said. "The president receives an abundance of mail, all of which is sorted off-site. The letter from The Angler is still there for further inspection. But they released the statue and delivered it here this morning."

We walked down a long corridor, past a bunch of fancy rooms that were named after colors and dead presidents. Then Ms. Lopez led us down some stairs and into...a bowling alley? It only had one lane, but still. I wondered if the White House had a game room, too. If I ever become president, I'm putting in a baseball field.

Besides the bowling lane, the room had a rack-thingy with a bunch of bowling balls on it, plus two chairs. Between the chairs was a giant sculpture of a fish. He was balancing on his tail, and it looked like he was guarding the place. Someone had tied a red scarf around his neck. Someone else had given him a purple and green bowling shirt.

"The guys in the mail room have been calling him Moby Dick, after the whale," Ms. Lopez said.

"Actually," said Nanny X, "I believe this is a wolffish."

The fish didn't look like a wolf or a whale. He looked like Jabba the Hutt, only sadder. And fishier. "Look at that attention to detail," Nanny X said. "He's magnificent."

She plucked a fishing lure off her hat—the blue minnow, not the purple one. "Extra camera," she explained. I put up two fingers and gave the sculpture bunny ears, as Nanny X pressed down on a fin and clicked. I wasn't tall enough to reach his head, though; instead they came out of his right fin. Nanny X pressed down on the camera's fin and clicked. "I'm sending this straight to our crime database," she said. My bunny-ear fingers were going to be famous. I hoped NAP had a sense of humor. Because if they didn't, my sister was going to kill me.

Just then a man walked into the room and held a whispered conference with Ms. Lopez. He left her with a plastic bag that contained a note.

"From The Angler," she said. "And this one didn't go through our sorting center. Somehow it landed here."

Ms. Lopez handed the bag to Nanny X, who read out loud, right through the plastic:

It has begun.
I've taken one.
(Plus Montauban's thumb.)
Install my fish
Or you will wish
You had.

It was signed *The Angler.*

Howard loped over to the bowling balls. He rolled a red one down the lane, using two hands instead of one. The pins blasted to the sides. Strike!

Howard clapped for himself and nodded his head.

"Eeeeee," he said. I was pretty sure that was Howard's way of saying that The Angler had struck again.

"I must find out how this got through," Ms. Lopez said.

"And we must contact our other operatives," said Nanny X. I was pretty sure "operatives" meant my sister, Boris and Stinky. And Yeti, of course.

We grabbed Nanny X's diaper bag and Eliza's stroller and exited through the North Portico, which is a reading-connection word for a porch-y thing with columns.

We called Boris right away, with the diaper phone on speaker so I could hear, too.

"We received your photo of the sculpture," he said. "Mr. Huffleberger sees a definite similarity between The Angler's fish and the fish he saw at the Georgetown gallery. It wasn't the same fish, mind, so there are doubts. But they could have been created by the same artist."

"That's progress," said Nanny X.

"There's more," Boris said. "That painting that disappeared from the National Gallery? The museum is bringing in something to replace it this afternoon. I don't know what it is, but they're calling it a national treasure."

"We'd better get over there," Nanny X said. "Whatever it is, it's vulnerable."

13. Alison

Nanny X Knows Her Alphabet

Nanny X must not have skated to the gallery, because we beat her by a mile. Yeti thumped his tail outside the museum door and sat down beneath a sign that said Only Service Animals Allowed Inside.

"Can't we bring him in?" I asked.

"Not this time," Boris said. "There are delicate pieces inside. Yeti does not look so delicate. Let's wait for your nanny, and we will figure things out together."

I didn't want to figure things out together. I wanted to figure things out *first*. The last case had been ours until Jake got caught and Nanny X had to give herself up to save him. Then Boris had to come and help. NAP knew all about that. Maybe that was why they gave this case to Boris and Stinky first. Maybe that was why they waited so long to call us in, leaving me to focus on math instead of stopping The Angler from slicing the thumb off of *The Great Warrior of Montauban*.

I put my hands in my pockets to keep from biting the nails off of my own thumbs. That's when we saw a van on Constitution Avenue with its blinkers on.

"Looks like we had excellent timing," said Boris.

The van's back doors were open. The driver was in front, examining a flat tire.

"I can fix that," Boris said.

"Who are you? Triple A?"

Boris reached into one of his pockets and pulled out a pen.

Stinky, who is always willing to help people, grabbed it from him and stuck it in the tire, pressing on the cap with his thumb. *Click. Click.* It sounded sort of like our squirrel. Slowly the tire began to fill with air.

While Stinky was working on the tire, a man from the museum came out with a pile of paperwork and two assistants.

"Quite a welcoming committee," said the driver.

"For a work by Paul Revere?" said the museum man. "It's art and history combined. We should have fireworks." He followed the driver to the back of the van. I followed them, too. Inside was a giant crate, which was filled with bubble wrap and packing peanuts. The crate was open, and the packing peanuts spilled across the floor of the van like snow. Inside was what I guess was a pitcher, except that the top part was chewed up, as if it had been through the garbage disposal.

"How can you pour it without a handle?" I asked. But when I looked closer, I could see where the handle *used* to be. It was missing, like the Warrior of Montauban's thumb.

The museum man and his assistants went pale. So did the driver.

"*Security!*" they yelled.

"Twice in one day," moaned the museum man. "I'm not going to have a job tomorrow. I'm not."

A security guard reached us just as Nanny X showed up with my sister and brother and Howard. I may have mentioned that my brother loves initials. So does Nanny X. The security guard used so many, it was like he was speaking another language.

"I'm the ASO," he said. He didn't seem upset like everyone else. He seemed kind of happy. "Looks like we have a CODA. We'll need to put out an APB for whoever damaged our AOI." He looked at his watch. "ETA 1400. AAR, I'm calling in the FBI. It's been one HOAD."

Jake translated ASO, which stood for assistant security officer, and APB, which meant all-points bulletin. The security officer told us CODA stood for Case of Damaged Art, and AOI stood for Artwork of Interest. If you ask me, he made both of those up. HOAD, apparently, stood for Heck of a Day.

"Alphabet soup," Stinky said, shaking his head. The only acronym he knew was EPA, for Environmental Protection Agency. And NAP, of course. He smiled, a slow, real smile. I wanted to smile back, but instead I got down to business.

"How can you put out an APB on a person when you don't know what he or she looks like?" I said. The only thing Mr. Huffleberger told us about Ursula, who was our main suspect, was that she had brown hair. Do you know how many people in Washington, D.C., have brown hair?

"Eeeee, eeee," said Howard, who had brown hair. So did Boris and Stinky.

"I suppose we should check for prints," the officer said. "But I'm betting we won't find any."

I noticed what looked like silver sawdust on the floor of the van near the crate. I decided to keep that particular clue to myself, which was easy to do since Jake kept talking about the pitcher.

"Was it really made by Paul Revere?" he asked the museum man.

"Yes," said the man, looking a little sick.

"Didn't he make others?" he asked.

"Not like this," said the man, looking sicker.

I wondered what would be next. My dad's museum, where he worked when he wasn't across the state taking care of my grandmother, was filled with natural treasures. My favorites were the rocks and minerals on the second floor—especially azurite and malachite, which looked like they were made of seawater. They reminded me of the geode Stinky had given me when we solved our last case. I hoped the rocks were safe. And what about the Hope Diamond? And my own art? It was on display back near the Smithsonian Castle. It wasn't a national treasure, but it could be some day, if art turned out to be my true calling. And if The Angler didn't get there first.

14. Jake

Nanny X Holds the Bag

Stinky is in fifth grade, which means he's always hungry. I guess Boris is used to that, because he had some granola bars in one of his pockets and he gave them to us. They weren't even the store-bought kind; they were homemade. Stinky said there were lentils in there, because they're Boris's trademark, but I couldn't taste them. Howard's snack was another banana from Nanny X. It was a little squished from being in the diaper bag, but Howard didn't mind.

Boris volunteered to stay outside the museum with the animals and the stroller. "I want to help them search the van for clues," he said. "You never know what they'll miss."

The rest of us went through the museum doors.

"I'm sorry, ma'am," a guard said to Nanny X. "You'll have to check that." He pointed at the diaper bag. I don't think he was worried about weapons like they were at the White House; he was just afraid she'd knock it into a piece of artwork. I could see where just having a bunch of pockets was handier.

Nanny X handed me a pacifier. "Don't pull on it," she said. She handed Ali a copy of *Hop, Sweet Bunny,* which I guess was the sequel to *Moo, Sweet Cow.* "Don't open it," she said.

Then she took her bag to the coat-and-bag check. She came back with a ticket that said No. 27, which was easy to remember because that's the number on the back of my baseball jersey.

"This way," she said, walking at Nanny X speed down one of the hallways. I guess she knew exactly where the portrait of George Washington should have been hanging.

As we walked, we played a speed version of our favorite art-museum game, where you try to name the art before you get close enough to see what it's really called. It was more fun to guess than it was to look at the actual art. You could win if you kept guessing *Untitled,* but that was cheating. I wished The Angler had gone after a treasure from the Air and Space Museum; that would have been a better place to search.

Finally we reached the room where Salvador Dali's portrait of George Washington had been hanging. There was a gold frame on the wall. Inside the frame there was nothing at all.

Some metal poles and police tape made a square fence around the area in front of the frame. Next to it was a small black plate that explained where the painting had been found, and that Salvador Dali was a surrealist, which, according to Nanny X, meant that George Washington had cherry blossoms growing out of his ears. Plus, his nose was melting.

After we stared at the empty frame for a while, Ali looked down and did a little sucky thing with her breath.

"What?" said Stinky.

She looked like she couldn't decide whether or not to tell us. But Nanny X nodded her head. "Go ahead, Alison," she said, which made me think that Nanny X had noticed the thing, too.

Ali squatted on the floor to look more closely, so we all squatted down. "Well, it's sawdust," she said. "Or maybe something-else dust. It was in the van, too, only in the van it was silver."

My powers of observation needed more training, because I had missed that dust. I wished I had a magnifying glass, but all I had were my regular eyes. Still, I could see that the dust was not just brown or white, but lots of other colors. A little red. A little pink. A little green.

Eliza got down on her stomach. She didn't seem interested in Ali's sawdust, but she reached under the yellow tape and grabbed something with her fingers. I wasn't sure how she even saw it: a screw, like the kind my dad is always replacing in his glasses. Only this one was emerald-colored.

"Achy!" she said, which is her name for me. "Coo!" She sounded like a little bird—a little bird that was saying "clue."

Nanny X put it in one of her evidence bags.

I looked around the floor of the gallery, but didn't see anything else. We walked back toward the exit in the East Building, and I kept looking down. That's why I saw a wadded-up piece of paper on the floor. I picked it up, hoping it wasn't somebody's old gum, and uncrumpled it. Inside was a poem, like the one we'd seen at the White House.

I started small
With Sal and Paul
But the next one's tall.
Install my fish
Or you will wish
That you people had listened to me
when you got my first note.

I showed it to Nanny X as we stood underneath the Calder mobile. I hoped it wouldn't fall on her, like Montauban's thumb.

While we were reading, Eliza pointed at the exit. I followed her finger to the dark squirrel that seemed to be looking into the museum from the outside. Ali came up behind me.

"No way," she said.

"Way."

"That rogue!" said Nanny X. She moved her arms in a karate pose—"*Kee-yah!*" she yelled—and charged toward the revolving doors. We followed her, but even though we exited, Nanny X kept revolving. She stopped when she got back inside the museum. I could see her waving her slip with the "27" on it in her karate-chop hand as she headed back to find the coat check.

15. Alison

Nanny X Skates Right By

It was like we were on one of those TV shows where everybody falls out of the closet at the same time. Jake, Stinky and I burst through the revolving door carrying Eliza. But the squirrel had disappeared again. I looked left and right and even up. Nothing. It felt like third grade when I'd kicked the ball in the wrong direction during a soccer game. I thought I was clear for my first goal, but it turned out I was just helping the other team. This time I wasn't helping anybody. Except maybe the squirrel.

"*Boris?*" Stinky yelled. I guess he thought it was okay to use our outside voices now that we were outside the museum. But everyone around us was still using their inside voices. They looked up when Stinky yelled, except for some lady who was staring at a video game. "Where are you? Boris? Boris!"

He came over with Howard, Yeti and the stroller.

"What did you find?" he asked.

"The squirrel," Jake said. "But he got away. Did you see him?"

"I did not see your squirrel," he said. "But I did find some mysterious dust." Boris has lived in the U.S. since he was a little kid, but he was born in Jamaica so sometimes he has a leftover accent. Words like "mysterious" sound more musical when he says them.

"There was some under the missing picture in the museum," I told him. "It was mysterious, too; not like regular sawdust."

"Paper?" Boris asked. "Or perhaps canvas?"

We nodded.

"That means that painting did not disappear, like the headline said, eh?" said Boris.

"No," Jake said. "It means it was destroyed."

"And our No. 1 suspect?" he asked.

"Still Ursula," I told him. "She's our only suspect. Unless you count the squirrel."

"Because she sculpts fish and smeared salmon pâté on our reviewer friend."

"He's not a friend," Stinky reminded Boris.

"No," Boris said. "Not of ours and not of Ursula's."

That made me remember something. "Wait a minute. Mr. Huffleberger said he'd seen her work before, a long time ago, at a fair. They may not be friends, but they must have met. At least once."

Boris nodded, slowly, and pulled his phone out of his pocket. He punched in the names "Ursula" and "Bartholomew Huffleberger."

Two articles flashed onto the screen. One was the review we'd already seen in *Artsy Bartsy*. The other was a 1974 article from the *Calvert City Messenger*. The article said that Ursula Marie Noodleman was the first-place winner in the county fair's painting category for ages twelve and under. She also took first place in the electronics competition, and she won third place for her goat in the juniors division. Mr. Huffleberger was only listed once, in the twelve-and-under painting category. "Honorable mention," it said.

Mr. Huffleberger and Ursula had known each other a long time ago because Ursula *had beaten him.*

"I'll bet he couldn't wait for the chance to give her a bad review," I said.

Jake nodded. "It was revenge."

"And now," said Stinky, picking up the story, "it's Ursula's turn to strike back."

"That's what she's been doing all day," I said. "That's what she's still doing." We just needed to figure out where she'd strike next.

Yeti barked at a squirrel running across the sidewalk. It was light gray instead of dark brown like our squirrel, so Yeti was the only one who wanted to chase it. Then we heard Howard's "Eeee!"

He'd spotted a squirrel, too, with dark fur and sad eyes. And this time it *was* the squirrel we were looking for. That meant it wasn't just a coincidence that he was hanging out at the sculpture garden when Montauban lost his thumb, or that we'd seen him at the museum when something had eaten half of a pitcher by Paul Revere. That squirrel and Ursula were working together. Jake's *Freaky Facts* book was right: Squirrels could be trained for espionage. Or destruction.

"Let's go!" I said.

"But Nanny X is still in the museum unchecking her bag," Jake said.

"She'll catch up," Boris said, putting Eliza in the stroller. "She's very spry."

So was the squirrel. Soon we were passing my dad's museum—Hooray, the squirrel had left it alone!—but we were heading for the Museum of American History, which was full of treasures, too. I didn't know if any of them counted as tall, like the treasure The Angler threatened to attack next. But they were all in danger.

I was still holding onto *Hop, Sweet Bunny*, the book Nanny X had given me. It was my only weapon. I pulled back the book's cover, which showed an angelic bunny dancing in a field of carrots. It screamed, twice as loud as *Moo, Sweet Cow*. It screamed like that bunny was being chased around the Beltway by a three-hundred-pound fox.

Everyone around us froze and covered their ears. Birds flew out of trees. A squirrel (not ours) dropped the french fry he was carrying.

But the squirrel we were chasing didn't stop or flinch. The squirrel we were chasing kept running.

Jake pulled out his stink-bomb pacifier. He squeezed the nib and threw it. Hard-boiled-egg smoke poured out. People's hands moved from their ears to their noses. But the stink bomb didn't stop the squirrel, either.

Jake and Stinky were huffing from running. So was Yeti.

One person was not huffing. And that was Nanny X. She'd put on her pink bunny slippers again, and now she was gliding past us with her elbows out, like she was practicing for the roller derby. She sailed through the stinky smoke just in time to see the squirrel ignore the No Animals sign and sneak through the museum door with a family of six.

This time Nanny X ignored the No Animals sign, too. By the time we caught up with her, she'd already changed back into her black Pilgrim shoes, flashed our badges at the guard and motioned us to follow her inside.

"Why didn't you just do that at the art gallery?" I asked.

"It didn't feel like as much of an emergency," she said.

"Mergenthee," said Eliza. It was the longest word she'd ever said.

"Exactly," said Stinky.

The squirrel had left the lobby, so we split up again to look for him.

"We meet back here in ten minutes," Nanny X said, pointing to a circle in the floor design.

"What if we don't find him by then?" asked Jake.

"Then another treasure," said Nanny X, "will have bitten the dust." The expression had a whole new meaning now.

Jake headed downstairs toward the trains, which are his favorite part of the museum. Nanny X and Eliza went with him, while Boris and a not-so-delicate Yeti headed for the Star-Spangled Banner. Maybe that counted as tall. Boris had Yeti's leash wrapped tightly around his wrist. "Keep that tail under control," Boris told Yeti. "No wagging until we're back outside."

Stinky and I took Howard and tried to decide between Lincoln's hat (which might count as tall), the first ladies' gowns (which could count as tall, too) and Dorothy's ruby slippers (not tall but very popular). What would attract a squirrel most? What would attract The Angler?

Then we saw a sign with a woman holding an enormous fish. "That's it," I said. "Julia Child's Kitchen."

Julia Child was a famous TV chef back when my grandmother was learning to cook. She was at least six feet tall.

We hurried downstairs to the exhibit. There he was! Julia Child's kitchen was mostly closed off by plastic, but a panel was missing, and the squirrel considered that an invitation to climb on top of Julia's counter, right next to the sink. He was holding a fake grape.

"We could jump it," Stinky said. Howard nodded. I'll bet he wished he had Julia Child's recipe for bananas flambé. I wished I had something—anything—to stop that squirrel.

And then I realized that I did. My pockets weren't as deep as Boris's and I didn't have as many of them, but there was some fishing line and thread in there, from when I was tying flies. I had a tiny weight, too, the size of a pebble. I threaded the fishing line through the weight and twirled it for a second, like a bola.

Then I loosened my grip and let the weight fly. It wrapped around the squirrel's tail. Maybe my true calling was being a cowgirl.

As the fishing line went tight, a couple of ladies who had been admiring Julia's pots screamed. I thought the squirrel would break the line and run away, but that's when Howard ran right into the exhibit. He took one of Julia Child's copper sauté pans off of the wall and conked the squirrel over the head with it. He brought the squirrel over to us. It was still kicking. Stinky wrapped some more fishing line and my black thread around its arms and legs. I tied the knots.

"It could have rabies!" shouted one of the women.

"It's a robot," Stinky said, showing off the metal underneath the fur.

But how would a robot know its way around the Museum of American History?

I thought about the drone that had brought Howard to us. It worked two ways, according to Nanny X: Remote programming and remote control. Someone must be controlling the squirrel.

My mind flashed back to the woman who'd been playing the video game outside the museum. Only now I was pretty sure it wasn't a video game. And I was pretty sure of something else, too: The woman was Ursula.

This time she hadn't left us an almost decent rhyming note, but maybe that was because she hadn't had the chance yet. The Angler was on the move. And so were we.

16. Jake

Nanny X Learns Some History

The squirrel wasn't near the trains or the 1903 Winton, which was the first car ever driven all the way across the United States. I figured he wouldn't be too hard to find, though. Someone would see him and scream. But all I heard was the recording of the train whistle.

Then I heard another sound, like lava bubbling. Nanny X pulled out her diaper phone and opened a text message from NAP: "New fish. Fountain near Castle. Go."

I had never noticed a fountain by the Smithsonian Castle. Nanny X said that was because it was small, and there usually weren't any fish in it, not even goldfish. I wondered if that meant we were going after another robot. And if this time it was going to eat more than Eliza's coloring-book pages.

Nanny X called Boris and told him to wait for Ali and Stinky at the meeting spot in the lobby. Then they would join us at our new meeting place. (Actually, what she told him was that we would "rendezvous" near the Castle fountain. I wasn't sure "rendezvous" counted as a reading-connection word, because I'd never seen it in my reading.)

We took off for another round of fishing. I saw a woman standing outside the museum, playing some sort of video game. We'd seen her before, by the art gallery. She didn't notice anything around her, like the fact that our nice day was turning cloudy.

Eliza looked at the sky. "Uh-oh," she said.

I was getting tired of being paired up with Nanny X and my little sister all the time. But then I got a reward. As soon as we crossed onto the sidewalk on the Mall, Nanny X pulled out her bunny slippers and offered them to me.

"These are *arctic*," I said, pulling off one of my wet socks.

"Hyperborean," said Nanny X.

"Hyper—?"

"From the land beyond the north wind. I think that would count as cool. But be careful," she added. "We don't want any more broken legs."

I took off my other shoe and sock, and put my wrinkly feet into the softest slippers I'd ever worn. Then Nanny X helped me up, and I headed for the Castle.

The crowd was thinning out, now that it was getting cloudy, so there weren't many people to avoid. I led us around the building and into the courtyard on the other side.

Fast. Faster. Fastest.

"To the left, Jake Z," Nanny X called. I curved around.

The fountain was up ahead, between the Castle and the Arts and Industries Building. Fortunately my skating was way better than my swimming. I skated around two little kids and aimed for the fountain. But there was one thing I couldn't remember: how to slow down. It had something to do with the direction you pointed your toes. In? Out?

The fountain was getting closer.

"*In!*" yelled Nanny X. "You point your toes *in!*"

I changed the direction of my feet, but I wasn't fast enough.

Bam. I plowed right into the fountain. My knees went kind of numbish and my arms went into the water. At least the bunny slippers were still dry.

Since I had a close-up view of the fountain, I saw the fish right away. It looked almost identical to the fish we'd caught in the Potomac, only this one was kind of greenish, like the water, instead of red.

This time we knew exactly what to do. I took off the bunny slippers while Nanny X took a hook from her hat and added a little bit of fishing line. Then she borrowed a small piece of paper from Eliza's coloring book and baited the hook.

"You may do the honors," she said.

I dangled the line in the water.

Chomp.

I wondered what Ethan would think if I brought Eliza's coloring book with us the next time we went fishing. Nanny X didn't cut the fish open when I reeled it in, which made Eliza happy. Instead, our nanny poked the fish right in the eye. The tail stopped moving.

"I found an off switch!" she said. "That was almost too easy. The fish just doesn't seem as smart as that squirrel."

"Fish have smaller brains," I said.

Her eyebrows came together. "Maybe the fish were a prototype. An early version. Maybe they really aren't as smart."

Nanny X stuck the fish in her diaper bag. While we waited for Ali to meet us, we walked across the garden to see her painting, which was on display with a bunch of other artwork by fifth graders. Ali's portrait of Yeti was set up on an easel. His paws were on a screen door. I thought he looked like he was waiting for us to get home from school. I also thought he looked hungry.

Wait a minute: *I thought* he looked hungry. I *thought*.

What about the squirrel? Was it thinking, too? Or was somebody else doing the thinking for it? Somebody who was programming it, or maybe even using a remote control, like with Nanny X's drone?

An image of the video-game-playing lady sneaked into my brain again. She hadn't looked up when Stinky was yelling at the art museum. She hadn't looked up when we went running to the Castle. Maybe she hadn't looked up because she was busy trying to make a squirrel destroy the world.

"I think I know where Ursula is," I said.

We rushed back to the Mall, but the video-game lady had moved on. Nanny X grabbed her baby-powder spyglass. She looked both ways. Finally she focused on a giant building with a green dome on it: the National Museum of Natural History—my dad's museum.

"There she is," she said. She handed the glass to me and I peeked through it in time to see Ursula—or the lady we thought was Ursula—on the museum steps. The lens was so powerful, I could even make out a small beetle on the step beside her.

17. Alison

Nanny X Sets the Trap

We met Boris in the lobby and headed outside. Stinky held on to the fishing line with the squirrel dangling from the end of it. It swung back and forth when he walked. Its sad squirrel eyes looked even sadder. Anybody watching us would think it was dead.

We'd just started walking across the Mall when a park ranger stopped us.

"What in the Sam Hill do you think you're doing?" he said.

"Going to the Castle," said Stinky. He added a "sir" for extra politeness.

"I'm not even going to ask if you have a hunting permit," the ranger said. "Even with a permit, there's no hunting allowed."

"Hunting?" Stinky's mouth dropped open a little. The only thing he had ever hunted for was litter to pick up, and maybe some worms for compost. "We weren't hunting."

"No trapping," added the ranger. "No fishing."

Stinky held the squirrel right in front of the ranger's face, which got all scrunched up, like he smelled something bad. I guess I'd make a face like that, too, if I thought someone was waving a dead squirrel at me.

"It's mechanical," Stinky explained. "It isn't real."

The ranger reached out and flicked the squirrel. Even with the fur, it made a dull clanging sound. It swung back and forth, like a pendulum. I wanted to point out that the ranger could be getting fingerprints all over our evidence, but he took his fingers away.

He looked at Yeti for a minute, and then his eyes went to Howard. "Do you have a license for that?" he said.

"We do," Boris said. He pulled out his own badge. I hoped it would be enough, since Nanny X seemed to have everybody else's.

"Well," said the ranger. He didn't seem to know what to say after that, so Boris made a suggestion.

"Perhaps we should put our squirrel in a bag. That way we won't frighten the tourists."

The ranger looked grateful. "Just what I was going to suggest," he said. "Bag it. Carry on."

We stuffed the squirrel into a green nylon sack that Boris had in one of his pockets, and moved on to find Nanny X at the fountain. I was glad we had been reassigned to the Castle. That meant I could finally see my painting of Yeti.

Just then, a big drop of rain landed on my forehead.

"My painting!" I said.

I took off as the rain started falling even harder.

When we reached the exhibit, Mrs. Bonawali, our art teacher, was trying to cover up the artwork with a plastic sheet. "This was not in the forecast," she said.

Boris was craning his neck, looking all around for the

fountain and for Nanny X, but he took out a rain poncho and handed it to me. I put it over the Yeti painting, which had only gotten a little smeary near the tail. That's when I noticed the purple ribbon that meant fourth place.

Stinky had a piece in the exhibit, too, a mosaic he'd made out of lentils and other kinds of beans. But when Boris handed Stinky a poncho to put over his project, we saw a squirrel sitting on the easel, nibbling on the lentils.

From the way it was holding its head, it didn't look like a robot squirrel, either.

"I'm sorry, Daniel," Boris said, putting a hand on Stinky's head. Daniel was Stinky's real name. "At least we know he has good taste."

Stinky didn't look even a little upset. "And at least beans are natural," he said. "It's better for him than the other food he's probably finding around here."

Then I noticed something else on Stinky's artwork: a red ribbon, for second place. He'd beaten me, just like Ursula had beaten Mr. Huffleberger. But I could still beat him by finding more clues first.

I was working very hard on not being jealous when Stinky gave me his poncho. "I don't want to bother the squirrel," he said. I think he still felt bad that the robot squirrel got clobbered with the sauté pan.

I almost said no. But then the rain started coming down harder and I pulled it on. I looked like a dandelion, but at least I was dry. If there were ribbons for junior agents, I'll bet Stinky would have gotten a blue one. He'd get a blue one if there were ribbons for friends, too.

We still didn't see Nanny X or Jake or Eliza anywhere, even though they'd left way before we had. We went over to the fountain, which was pretty small. There were lots of ripples from the raindrops hitting the water. But we didn't see a fish. Maybe my brother had caught it already.

Boris led us back to the Mall side of the Castle. He spotted two people in the distance, running at top speed with a stroller. They stopped running, and Boris's phone rang. He held it to his ear, but we could still hear it when Nanny X said, "We've got her. We've got The Angler."

18. Jake

Something's Bugging Nanny X

"Got her" was an exaggeration. What Nanny X should have said was that we "possibly almost cornered her." Or "We see her!" That would have worked.

Because we did see The Angler. She was still standing on the top step of the Museum of Natural History as the rain fell down around her. And she was studying the screen on what was not a video game, but a remote control, just like I'd guessed.

At first I thought we should just go up behind and grab her, but we didn't know if she had any weapons. Plus, she had threatened the president of the United States. And even though she had threatened to destroy things and not people, once you start threatening destruction, it's probably hard to know when to stop. Nanny X's computer database—before it got destroyed—hadn't said "Armed and Dangerous." It hadn't mentioned Ursula at all. But there could have been an update.

"Approach with caution," Nanny X said, reading my mind. "Watch Eliza, Jake Z."

"What are you doing?" I whispered.

"I will engage." Nanny X adjusted the brim on her fishing hat. Then she reached into the diaper bag and pulled out a small, flowery umbrella. She popped it open and marched up the museum stairs. She actually marched, like a band was playing "Stars and Stripes Forever." Because of the rain, the tourists were getting inside as fast as possible. No one was paying attention to us. I guess that's the best way to be inconspicuous: Conduct your most important operations when it's raining.

I know I'm in trouble when my mom calls me by my whole name, Jacob Zachary Pringle. So I wasn't surprised when Nanny X used Ursula's whole name, now that we knew it.

"Ursula Marie Noodleman?" she said.

The lady looked at us, and I could tell she hadn't expected anyone to come up with that. She seemed to notice the rain for the first time, too. She took a fishing hat out of her pocket and put it on.

"I believe," Nanny X continued, "that you and I share an affinity for fish."

"I love fish," Ursula said. "And other creatures. Bugs, for instance."

If Ursula liked bugs, she was in the right place. The top floor of the Museum of Natural History had an insect zoo. But Ursula didn't seem interested in the exhibit, which was partly sponsored by an exterminating company. It turned out she had brought bugs of her own—beetles. Not that we needed more of them. According to my *Freaky Facts* book, there are more beetles than any other type of bug in the world.

Ursula's beetles were about the size of a half dollar and almost as flat. Some of the shells were green, like emeralds—and like the tiny screw Eliza had found at the art museum. Some were black.

You might think: What could a bug do? The answer is: a lot. For one thing, it could sneak through a museum door a lot more easily than a squirrel. Plus, beetles can chew.

Even if they didn't have brains as big as a squirrel—or a fish—they had Ursula at the controls. They could chomp on a painting, or the Easter Island statue, or the fur on the Neanderthals in the Prehistoric Man exhibit. They could destroy things.

Nanny X walked up a few more steps so she and Ursula were even. "You've brought some visitors to the museum, I see," she said, nodding at the bugs, which were getting rained on with the rest of us. I thought that was a weird word choice—"visitors"—as if the bugs were going upstairs to hang out with the hissing cockroaches.

"Just one is exploring the museum at the moment," said Ursula. "Sometimes one is all it takes."

If that was true, I thought, somebody had to find it.

My brain ping-ponged back and forth. *Ping*: A bug was already inside. *Pong*: Ursula was outside. *Ping*: The bug was small. *Pong*: It could still go *chomp*. What if the bug was chomping mummies in the Ancient Egypt exhibit *right now*?

I grabbed Eliza and we ran inside to search for that bug. This was where our dad worked. I'll bet even Nanny X didn't know the museum as well as we did. I'll bet Ursula didn't, either. I tried to guess where the bug would go. What was the most valuable thing in the museum? What was a national treasure?

So far she'd taken the Warrior of Montauban's thumb, a painting of George Washington and a pitcher by Paul

Revere. But she'd said she was going taller, which meant bigger.

The museum had lots of big things, starting with the African elephant near the front. We didn't see the beetle there. We peeked into the marine hall. Nope. Then I thought about the biggest things in the museum: the dinosaurs. They were big in size, plus they were popular.

I wanted to look at the T. rex, but Eliza toddled over to the triceratops. "Dina-tore," she said. He wasn't the tallest dinosaur ever made, but he was taller than me. He was also about thirty feet long.

I put my hands on the railing and stood next to Eliza. I felt a tickle. Then—*ouch*—I felt a chomp. A beetle, like the ones we'd seen near Ursula, had bitten my pinky.

My mother doesn't like us to kill bugs, except for mosquitoes. Instead, she asks us to "escort them outside." I picked up the beetle the way you'd pick up a crayfish, holding my fingers behind the pinchy part.

"Come on, Eliza," I said.

We escorted the bug back to Nanny X.

19. Alison

Nanny X Learns About Insect Digestion

I am not afraid of worms, snakes, mice, rats, bats or raw chicken, but bugs have freaked me out ever since Jake told me, during a previous visit to the museum, that there are more than ten quintillion insects in the world at any given time. There were only about twenty bugs outside the museum when we found Nanny X, but they were still disturbing, even though none of them was actually moving. The only bug that was moving so far was the one inside the museum, with my brother and Eliza.

"You know," said Stinky, who was probably sorry he'd given me the rain poncho, "with global warming there's going to be a major increase in the number of insects."

More than ten quintillion? But I was not going to run screaming down the stairs in front of Stinky. Yeti looked like he wanted to run, though. He has not liked bugs since his flea problem.

"The population has already grown," said a woman who had to be Ursula. She looked at her own bugs—kind of fondly, I thought. Her hair was brown, pulled back in a braid that poked out from underneath her fishing hat, which was like the one Nanny X wore except it was green instead of orange and it didn't have as many fishhooks in it.

Ursula hit a button on her remote, and the bugs near her feet began to move. They fanned out in different directions, some going toward the museum and some going away from it.

Nanny X took her umbrella and pointed it at one of the bugs. The umbrella didn't fly or talk, like Mary Poppins's umbrella. Instead, it shot out a blurp of clear liquid, the queen of all raindrops. The blurp hit the bug, which struggled for a minute, like it was dizzy. Then it straightened up and kept walking.

"Stop," said Ursula. She was talking to Nanny X, not the bug.

But Nanny X shot another blurp as the rain continued to fall. "It's supposed to be sticky," she said. "It's supposed to trap them like flypaper."

"The rain must be counteracting the stickiness," Boris said.

It was hard to believe my special-agent training was coming to this, but I couldn't think of what else to do. I walked up to the bug nearest to me and stomped on it. Tiny screws and mechanical pieces came spurting out of the side.

Stinky and Boris went after the bugs, too. So did Howard. Yeti stayed close to Boris but didn't attack anything. Nanny X reached into her diaper bag and pulled out an industrial-strength nasal aspirator. Nasal aspirators are what you use to suck the snot out of babies' noses when they are too young to blow properly. Jake called them "booger suckers." This one had a wide opening at the end, so when Nanny X squeezed the bulb part and let go, it slurped the beetle right inside.

"You are destroying my *art*," Ursula said.

"What about you?" said Nanny X as she sucked up another bug, and then another and another. "What have you destroyed?"

My brother came out of the museum then with my sister. In his hand he was holding a small black beetle. He ran down the steps and stood next to me and Stinky. Boris and Yeti and Nanny X came over to us, too. So did Howard.

We fanned out on the same step, side by side, like a team. Ursula had one last beetle near her foot. She reached down to catch it—and save it—and when she did, Nanny X lunged.

She twisted Ursula's arm behind her back and hand-cuffed her with a teething ring. She attached the other cuff around her own wrist.

"Art is about creating," said Nanny X. "Not destroying." She pulled out her diaper phone and pressed a button. "X, reporting in," she said. "We've got her."

I'd heard that before. But this time it was true. We'd caught The Angler, squished a bunch of bugs and saved a lot of national treasures from destruction. We hadn't saved all of them, though. I didn't know what NAP would have to say about that. Would we get another case after this one?

"You know," Jake told Urusla as the rain eased up and the sun started to look out on us again, "I thought your fish sculpture was very realistic. And your squirrel is totally tundra." Leave it to my brother to be polite to a criminal. He was right, though.

"You mean you think I'm good?" Ursula said. She didn't

mean "good person," which was in question at the moment. She meant "good at art."

"Yes," said Jake.

"Yes," Stinky and I agreed.

Jake frowned. "I'm not so sure about your poetry, though," he said. "Plus, you said you were going after something tall. None of the national treasures you picked was really very tall."

Ursula froze, her eyes wide. "But I did try to destroy a tall thing," she said. "Washington, D.C.'s tallest lawn ornament. It was the obvious choice."

We all looked down the Mall and saw it towering in the distance. The Washington Monument. Of course.

"It looks okay from here," I said.

Nanny X pulled out her baby-powder spyglass. She turned the dial. Then she turned it again, three more times. She looked at Ursula. "Hand me that remote," she said.

"They don't work with my remote," Ursula said. "They're automated. They just chew."

Nanny X ran to the curb at Nanny X speed. She whistled for a pedicab, but none came. I guess they didn't like the weather. Then she spied a row of Segways leaning against the wall. The owners must have gone somewhere to get out of the rain, which had now stopped completely.

"Mergenthee," said Eliza.

"Emergency," agreed Nanny X. She pulled a card out of her bag and handed it to Boris. "Congratulations!" it said. "Your _____ has been borrowed by a Top Secret Government Agency. It will be returned immediately after _____. Thank you for your cooperation."

Boris took a pencil out of his pocket and filled in the blanks: *Segway/We save the Washington Monument.* He attached the card to the wall above the Segways.

Nanny X unhooked Ursula's handcuffs. She handed her the helmet that was hanging from the handlebars. "Climb on."

"Us too?" I said.

"You too." Nanny X bent down and slid on her bunny slippers. They were still miraculously fuzzy, even after the rain and a day on the streets of D.C.

Boris gave us a Segway lesson. "Lean forward to go. Pull back to stop—but not too far back or you'll go in reverse. And don't let go of the handlebars."

"Got it!" yelled Jake.

"Got it," I said. I fastened my helmet and mounted my Segway, which I was way too young to drive unless the nation's most famous obelisk was in peril. I leaned forward. The wheels began to roll. I rolled, too, slow and shaky at first, but then straighter and faster as we followed our nanny to the Washington Monument. Ursula leaned right near Fourteenth Street and her Segway turned. Wait. That wasn't the way to the monument!

I'd been working on my whistling, which seemed like an important special-agent skill, so I puckered and made a sharp tweeting sound. Then more whistles joined mine. Jake and Stinky had been practicing, too. Nanny X skated back. She gave me Eliza's stroller as she and Boris made a fast turn. Yeti went with them, barking up a storm because, like I said, he's the best dog in the world. In seconds they returned with Ursula between them.

"I had to try," Ursula said.

We got back in our single-file line, with Nanny X and Eliza leading the way again. Then came Jake and me and then Stinky and Ursula. Boris was last, keeping an eye on all of us. He rang his bell as we passed pedestrians with the wind in our hair and a nasal aspirator full of destructive beetles in Nanny X's diaper bag.

20. Jake

Nanny X Goes Rock Climbing

Here are some facts about the Washington Monument: It is 555 feet high and it is made mostly out of marble. That means that most bugs leave it alone. Ursula's bugs were different. "They have small digestive systems," she said. "I'm sure they won't eat much."

But small cracks from an earthquake shut down the monument for a long time. Sometimes a little damage was all it took. Besides, Ursula's beetles (plus a squirrel) had eaten an entire portrait of George Washington and half of a pitcher by Paul Revere. They could do more than a little damage. They might even be able to topple the whole thing!

Howard put his hand on the cold marble and tried to climb. But there were no nooks to hold on to.

Nanny X tipped back her head and looked up. The bugs were walking around as though they owned the place. She plunged her hand into the diaper bag and pulled out two pairs of earrings with little pink balls on them. She clipped one pair to her ears and handed the other to Boris.

"We can keep in touch through these," she said.

Next she grabbed a tube of Boffo's Baby Butt Cream, which is not Eliza's usual brand for diaper rash. Nanny X squeezed some into each hand. She smeared some onto the bottom of her shoes, which had replaced the bunny slippers again.

She reached up with her right hand and touched the marble wall. Her hand stuck there, as if it were attached by suction. She reached up with her left hand. Slowly our nanny made her way up the side of the Washington Monument, just like a superhero.

"Be good to my bugs," Ursula called.

Nanny X reached the first beetle at about twenty feet up. *Shhhllllurp.* She sucked it into the nasal aspirator.

The next beetle was higher, and Nanny X kept climbing. We took turns watching through the spyglass. Ali took some pictures with Nanny X's diaper phone, to send to NAP. There was no way they would think she wasn't in special-agent condition now. Unless she fell.

Shhhllurp. Another bug went into the aspirator.

We could feel a crowd gathering around us. The flags that surrounded the monument whipped and fluttered as two park rangers came up behind us. "What's she doing?" one of them said.

"She can't do that," said the other.

"Yes," Boris said, "she can. She's with NAP."

He spoke into one of the earrings, which he'd fastened to his shirt collar. "X, are you okay?" he said. "Can you read me?"

"Loud and clear," said our nanny.

And that's when my brand-new powers of observation

spotted something through the spyglass: One beetle, faster than the rest, had made it more than halfway up the monument. Nanny X would have to climb a long way to get it.

I passed the glass to Ali, whose powers of observation are better than mine, and she spotted something else: a small hole in the side of the aspirator. The beetles were eating their way through.

"Boris to X. We have a problem. Two problems. Do you read?"

"I read," said Nanny X. "What problems?"

He told her.

"If I get you the aspirator, can you plug the hole?" asked Nanny X.

"I think so," Boris said. "I'm coming up."

"I've got this," said Nanny X. "Watch Ursula and the children. Send Howard for the beetles."

In no time, Howard had butt cream on his hands and feet. He climbed straight to Nanny X. He was a much faster climber than she was. His body didn't shake. He grabbed the nasal aspirator in his mouth and climbed back down to us. He put the aspirator on the ground near Boris's feet.

Stinky grabbed Nanny X's flowered umbrella, and was about to use it to squirt some goop inside the nasal aspirator.

"Wait!" Ursula said. "Don't destroy them. Please."

She pointed to her bag, which wasn't half as big as Nanny X's. Boris had taken charge of it, in case there were weapons inside. He reached in and pulled out a metal box.

"Won't they just eat through it?" I asked.

"The inside is curved," Ursula said. "They can't grab it with their teeth."

I figured the bugs were going to be taken away as evidence, so her artwork would be locked up for a while, but I guess that was easier than seeing them squished or covered in goop. Boris squeezed the bugs out of the aspirator and into the box. He slammed the lid down. Ursula wrapped the box with a chain and locked it. It shook a little, but she was right; they couldn't escape.

"Thank you," she said.

"Or course," Boris said. He handed the box to Stinky.

"Guard these," he added. Then he attached the teething ring hand cuff to Ursula's wrist. He attached the other half to the Segway, which was leaning against the flagpole.

Above us, the last bug was still free. Nanny X was still climbing. She was so high now that she looked like a bug herself.

Then she stopped. She pulled back her right leg and her body flailed around. Ali bit her fingernails. Through the earring on Boris's shirt, we heard Nanny X shout "*Kee-yah!*" She swung her right foot and kicked the beetle off the monument and into the sky.

"*Noooooooooooooo!*" screamed Ursula. She tried to move closer to the monument as the bug plummeted down, but she was handcuffed to the Segways. Ursula and the Segways fell over like dominoes. But that didn't stop her. At the last second, Ursula took off her fishing hat and held it out in her uncuffed hand.

Sshhhhhpppp. She snagged the bug just before it hit the ground. Forget about art. Ursula would have been an amazing baseball player. Except instead of the catch being an out, the catch meant her bug was safe.

We looked back up at Nanny X, who was making her way, slowly and steadily, down the side of the Washington Monument.

"How did I do?" she asked Boris when she reached the ground.

"Very spry," he said.

We waited for the Capitol Police to come and get Ursula. I felt kind of sorry for her. Destroying national treasures plus threatening the president was going to put her in jail for a long time, even if the only person she had hurt was me, when her bug bit my pinky.

"Perhaps you could teach art in prison," Nanny X said. "I hear it's very therapeutic."

I remembered Mr. Huffleberger's review, where he said she should go back to doing arts and crafts with the Girl Scouts. The other inmates weren't going to be Girl Scouts, but it sounded like a start. I wasn't sure what kind of art material they had in jail, but I hoped they had something she could sculpt with, even if it was just butter or mashed potatoes.

"One question," said Nanny X as the sirens came closer. "Why?"

It was a question I had, too. *Why threaten the president? Why destroy stuff?*

Ursula dropped her head so we could barely see her face. "I wanted my art to be appreciated," she said.

I didn't want to tell her, but that wasn't what was happening in the president's bowling alley.

"I can't believe you let a schlump like Huffleberger make you crazy," said Nanny X. "But if it makes you feel better, I think you made him a little crazy, too."

"My career peaked at the county fair," Ursula said. "But it's not over yet." She turned to Nanny X. "By the way," she said, "how high are your ceilings?"

*   *   *

Before Ursula got into the squad car, she arranged for Nanny X to take control of the fish statue. The police mumbled something about it being too big to keep in their evidence room anyway, and that photos would do until the trial. If they needed the statue in person, Nanny X said she'd be happy to bring it in.

I guess I knew what we'd be tying to the minivan instead of the canoe.

"You know something?" Ali said, after the police had taken Ursula away. "She's kind of a genius."

"An evil genius," I said.

"But maybe not forever," Stinky added. "You know something else? I'll bet we could find a way to use Ursula's bug power to save the world. We could set them loose in the dump and they could eat trash instead of art."

"That would take a lot of bugs," Ali said. "They only ate one painting—even if it was a surrealist painting. You remember what Ursula said about their digestion."

"I know," said Stinky. "But maybe we could change that."

Maybe we could change a lot of things.

We made it back to Lovett just in time for my baseball game. I'd been wet all day, so standing in the wet grass of left field didn't bother me.

It felt good to be part of two teams—my baseball team and my special-agent team. I wasn't sure I'd have time to keep doing both, but Nanny X told me about Moe Berg, who was a baseball player *and* a spy during World War II. Plus he was on quiz shows. I wonder if his specialty was knowing freaky animal facts?

My own secret-agent team watched me play from the stands. Nanny X even let Howard stay. He was still wearing Eliza's bonnet when he caught a foul ball in the third inning.

When the game was over, we all drove Howard back to the David T. Jones Primate Sanctuary in Nanny X's minivan. The giant fish sculpture was on top.

21. Alison

Nanny X Puts a Fork in It

My parents called to check on us during dinner, which was late because Jake's baseball game lasted forever. Stinky and Boris had come over, and we were eating hamburgers—the lentil kind, which weren't so bad with ketchup—and sweet-potato fries. For dessert we had soft molasses cookies, my grandmother's recipe.

"How's Grandma?" I asked my mother when it was my turn to talk.

"Home and hurting but hobbling around," my mother said. "Did you do anything special today?"

I chose my words carefully. "We caught a criminal who threatened the president of the United States with a statue of a wolf fish," I said. "That about sums it up."

"Alison," said my mother. "Let's not start."

"We went fishing and saw some art and the Washington Monument," I told her.

"I'm so glad Nanny X is teaching you about the finer things," my mother said.

I was glad, too. Of course, everybody has a different idea about the finger things.

To some people they are paintings.

To some people they are sculptures of fish.

To Stinky they are a clean planet, to Howard they are a bunch of bananas, and to Jake they are the sound of a baseball when you crack it with a bat.

And to me? To me, the finer things are running around Washington, D.C., chasing criminals with a nanny who wears mirrored sunglasses, a motorcycle jacket and pink bunny slippers that just happen to turn into roller skates.

Name the Artwork
By Alison and Jake Pringle

Look at a piece of art from a distance. Decide whether you think it's modern, ye olde, impressionistic or realistic. Give it a name. When you get closer, see how much of the name you got right.

If you guess the whole title right, it's ten points.

If you guess the idea of the title (like if you say *Galaxy* and the painting is really *Solar System* or you say Bronze Statue No. 5 but it's really No. 14) you get five points.

If you guess part of the title (like if you *Bronze Statue #3* but it's really *Bronze Statue #12*, or if you say *Girl with Trees* but it's really *Girl in Wind*), you get five points.

You are only allowed to guess *Untitled* twice per gallery visit.

Nanny X's Skating Tip No. 12: How to Stop

With your knees wide and over your feet, turn your toes in and squat low. Now dig hard with your edges (that's the sides of your wheels) and squeeze your thighs. That's a plow stop. The idea is to stop *before* you plow into somebody. Unless you happen to be in roller derby—which I am, Tuesday nights at eight.